SPIRIT SINGER

PRAISE FOR SPIRIT SINGER

"...a strong, well-written book with great adventure and sympathetic characters...fast-paced adventure, sword-play, ghostly help, kidnappings, automatons who serve pure evil, royalty, and brave commoners...It is about deception, both external and internal, in the eternal search for love and acceptance. It is about the need to accept oneself to be able to move forward and achieve great things and the need to be wise and discerning about others."

— LYNN (J.R.) WYTENBROEK,
CANADIAN LITERATURE MAGAZINE

"This is a fast-paced, spiritual quest book, full of narrow escapes, evil masquerading as good, good appearing in nasty people (just like in real life!), adventure, dreams, and bits of wisdom. The writing is spare and the words well-chosen, so that complex characters and interesting places emerge full-blown in the reader's mind, and the plot moves apace. I felt always in the story, and not a mere spectator/reader. Written for teenagers, but this fifty-something guy had a great time."

— DAVID WALTNER-TOEWS

"Clearly defined characters, setting, and plot carry a reader eagerly from page to page through adventure-filled chapters that deftly conclude with cliff-hangers…The plot is fast-paced and clever, the writing never disappoints, and the author clearly keeps his target audience in mind. A great read from start to finish."

— SHIRLEE MATHESON

"…a fun novel with engaging characters and having all the basic elements of a good fantasy…young readers would likely get much more out of this book in terms of good succinct plotting and writing than they'd ever be likely to from the droves of role-playing game tie-ins and fat fantasy trilogies."

— GEORGES T. DODDS, SF SITE

*"This book takes the reader on a magical journey to a mystical land…It is a quick, but very satisfying read; I spent any free time I had reading over the two days it took me to read the story. I recommend this book for anyone that is in the mood for an adventure…*Spirit Singer* definitely does not disappoint."*

— AMY MEHTA, MYSHELF.COM

SPIRIT SINGER

EDWARD WILLETT

SHADOWPAW
PRESS

SPIRIT SINGER

Published by
Shadowpaw Press
Regina, Saskatchewan, Canada
www.shadowpawpress.com
orders@shadowpawpress.com

Third edition
Revised by the author

First edition published 2002
by Awe-Struck E-books, Inc.

Second edition published 2012
by Tyche Books Ltd.

This edition copyright 2019
by Edward Willett
All rights reserved

ISBN 978-1-989398-00-5
Kindle ISBN 978-1-989398-01-2
Epub ISBN 978-1-989398-02-9

Cover design by Edward Willett

This book is dedicated to the memory of my father
James Lee Willett
1926-2002

CHAPTER 1

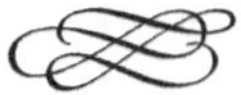

Something woke Amarynth in the small hours of the night.

It was dark as a cave inside her chamber, except for the faint bar of moonlight on the stones of the wall by the open door. For a moment, she blinked at that pale oblong, feeling the cool breath of a breeze against her cheek, wondering what had roused her.

Then she heard it again—a moan, from down the hallway. Her grandfather.

Amarynth threw aside the covers and reached for her long blue robe, donning it over the thin shift in which she slept. The moan came again as she stepped into the corridor, the smooth stone floor cold beneath her bare feet. She hurried its length, passing through pools of moonlight collected under the open skylights like puddles of rain.

Her grandfather's room was at the far end of the

corridor, past the library and the meditation chamber. Amarynth knocked gently. "Grandfather? Are you all right?"

For a moment, there was no answer; then she heard him moan again, his voice rising suddenly to a shout. "No! No! Stay away! *Stay away!*"

Amarynth opened the door and rushed in. Her grandfather sat upright in bed, eyes wide and staring, face pale in the darkness. "Leave me alone!" he cried.

She seized his shoulders. "Grandfather, wake up! Wake up! It's me, Amarynth!"

A shudder ran through his gaunt body, and suddenly his eyes focused on her. "Amarynth...?"

She felt the tension go out of him, and gently laid him back on his bed. "You were dreaming again," she said. "Shouting at someone to stay away."

"Not someone—some *thing*." He closed his eyes, rubbing his forehead with his gnarled hand. "The dreams are getting worse. I'm afraid..." His voice trailed off.

"Of what, Grandfather?"

His eyes snapped open. "I'm sorry I disturbed you. I'm all right now. Go back to bed."

"If only you'd tell me what you dream, maybe—"

"A dream is only a dream. It's not important. Now, go on. You need your sleep."

"But—"

"Amarynth."

She sighed. "Yes, Grandfather." With a backward glance she went out, closing the door behind her, then returned to her room. She draped her robe over the chair once more, but instead of going back to bed, went to the window and looked down the hill to the darkened village of Covedrift, two-score huts strung along a curving shingle beach. The cool night air caressed her skin and brought to her the quiet, unceasing murmur of the ocean.

The dreams had been troubling her grandfather for weeks, but she had never heard him cry out like that before, as though trying to drive something away. What did he see in the night? He would never tell her. Nor would he explain *why* he wouldn't tell her, almost as if he were protecting her from something. But from what? "I'm not a child anymore," she murmured to the night. "I don't have to be protected from bad dreams."

She crossed to the other window of her corner room and stared out over the ocean, almost calm this night, a gentle swell barely breaking against the rocks at the base of the cliff, sixty feet below her. The moon silvered what waves there were and gave a pale glow to a fine mist far out at sea, making the horizon indistinct, blending the ocean smoothly with the starry sky.

It will be good weather for the First Sailing, Amarynth thought. In just a few hours, as the sun rose over the distant inland mountains, the three young men who had turned seventeen in the past year would ascend to the tower, as their fathers had when they turned seventeen, so that her grandfather could forge the L ink that would draw their spirits back to Covedrift should they be lost at sea. Then they would set out in the boats they and their fathers had fashioned, to sail the deep alone for a day and a night. When they returned, they would be considered men, and would take their place in the fishing fleet.

Her mind drifted from her grandfather's dreams to Davin, one of the boys who would be making that climb to the tower in the morning. She smiled a little. Walking in the village a week ago, she had seen him watching her, as she had seen other boys watch other girls, and when she had come back from the market, arms laden with seaweed-wrapped fish, he had contrived to be in the road.

He hadn't said much—in fact, he'd seem tongue-tied by his own audacity—but he had carried her fish up the hill to the tower for her, and when she'd smiled her thanks he'd turned as red as the seaweed before stammering, "You're welcome," and almost running back to the village.

But at least he'd seen her as someone besides Spirit Singer Nikos's granddaughter, someday to be a Singer in her own right—as though that made her some kind of witch! Everyone else in Covedrift treated her with oh-so-careful respect.

When Davin and the others returned from their First Sailings, they would be full-fledged members of society.

When I make my solo journey, thought Amarynth, *when I become a full-fledged Spirit Singer, I'll be cut off from society forever.*

Suddenly chilled, she turned back to the warmth of her bed; but it was a long time before she slept.

She woke to the sound of trumpets. Outside her window the sky was greying with dawn, and looking out, she saw people already filling the streets of Covedrift, their laughter and shouting echoing up to the tower as they prepared to send off the three boys. The sight and sound of merriment brought back full-force the night's lonely thoughts.

"Are you up, Amarynth?" her grandfather called from down the hall.

"Yes, Grandfather!" she shouted back. Putting away her black mood, she hurriedly grabbed her ceremonial clothes from the rough-carved wardrobe by the door, dropping the long, sleeveless white robe over her head and belting it around her waist with a scarlet sash. Around her neck she placed her Emblem, a tear-shaped black stone the size of her thumb, strung on a golden chain, and on each wrist she clasped three thin, silver bracelets that jingled like bells as she moved. Finally, she slipped on her white sandals.

As she straightened, the sky suddenly tinged with red and the cheering died away. She looked out and saw three distant figures beginning the quarter-mile climb from the village to the tower.

Amarynth ran out of her room, not turning right down the hallway this time but instead going straight, down worn stone steps and through a blue velvet hanging into the Spirit Chamber, where her grandfather made ready for the Linking.

The long, narrow chamber had no windows; the only light came from the small fireplace to Amarynth's left and brass lamps hung on chains from the ceiling's smoke-stained beams. Blue-and-gold curtains covered the walls above heavy wooden benches. In the centre of the room stood an oblong dais of black stone, three feet high, between two simple chairs of dark wood. At the head of the dais stood a single bronze candlestick, its unlit white candle at eye level for her grandfather, who sat in one of the chairs, eyes closed, and fingertips pressed together.

Amarynth was shocked by how old he looked; the lines in his face seemed deeper, the flesh of his chin more sagging. Even his shoulder-length hair seemed whiter. He wore a golden robe, and around his neck hung his own Emblem; but unlike Amarynth's, his glowed a deep purple, and at its centre burned a spark of light.

She crossed to the dais and sat in the opposite chair. After a moment her grandfather's eyes opened and met hers. "Good morning," he said.

"Good morning." Amarynth gestured at the candle-stick. "I'm ready to help."

"I'm sorry, Amarynth. Not this time."

Amarynth stared at him. "But I've been studying for weeks. You said this is one of the most vital tasks of a Spirit Singer—"

"It is," said her grandfather. "And you will learn it, I promise. But not today. I will forge the Links alone."

"But Grandfather, you promised last week—"

"I've changed my mind." He closed his eyes again.

"Grandfather—"

Without looking at her, he said, "Please don't argue, Amarynth. I must concentrate. I suggest you prepare for your class. The children will be here shortly."

Amarynth, her lips pressed tightly together, rose from her chair and strode out through the curtained arch. There she banged her hand against the wooden banister of the stairs so hard it hurt and muttered a few words she had learned from the Covedrift fishermen.

Why? she thought angrily. *Why has Grandfather changed his mind?* She *knew* she could make the Link—she had read everything in the library on the subject, and they had practised over and over. Only four days ago, her grandfather had told her she was far more prepared than he had been when he had first assisted with a Linking. Now he refused to let her help. What had changed?

The dreams. It has to be the dreams. Grandfather is afraid of something—but what? And why should that make him mistrust me?

She had no answers, and at last she went to the classroom as her grandfather had suggested, going by way of the kitchen, where Marta, the village woman whose week it was to help at the Spirit Singer's tower, hummed as she kneaded dough. Amarynth snagged crusty bread and hard cheese from the pantry and chewed on them as she crossed the great hall, the rising sun casting bars of golden light through the eastern windows, high above the rock-ribbed walls.

The great hall's main doors of intricately carved black wood stood open. She passed through them into an antechamber, on the far side of which even larger iron-bound doors also stood wide, letting in light—and wind, Amarynth noticed, hearing it howl around the tower's high walls. *The First Sailing won't be so smooth after all,* she thought, and felt perversely pleased that someone else would also have problems this day.

Besides the doors leading into the great hall and those opening into the outdoors, there were two other exits from the antechamber, one a curtained arch into the Spirit Chamber, the other a narrow door into a small, square room, where Amarynth daily taught the village children reading, writing, history, and, most importantly, the teachings of the Master. Marta had already lit the fire and opened the shutters, Amarynth discovered when she looked in; there was really nothing for her to do there until the children arrived, and despite what her grandfather had said, she did not expect that to be for an hour, at least.

She went outside and leaned against the tower wall to finish her bread and cheese. As she took her last bite, the three village boys came over the crown of the hill, Davin lagging behind the other two. Their festival clothing of red, green, and blue wool and shining fish-leather only emphasized the paleness of their faces. Amarynth straightened quickly and nodded gravely as the first two passed her, bowing slightly and touching their fingers to their chests, then gave Davin a wink that brought a rush of blood to his cheeks but also earned her a tentative smile in return.

When the boys had entered the Spirit Chamber, she crossed the great hall again, went back through the kitchen to the stairwell, and finally peered into the Spirit Chamber through a narrow opening in the curtain covering the arch.

Her grandfather stood with his head bowed in prayer, his Emblem clenched in his right hand. When he raised his head, his face looked white and strained. He sat down in his chair and motioned the three boys forward, gesturing to them to sit on the dais in front of him.

Shifting the Emblem to his left hand, he reached out and touched each boy's forehead. At once their eyes closed. Amarynth's grandfather took a deep breath and closed his own eyes.

It appeared nothing was happening, but Amarynth knew better. Her grandfather had sent the boys' spirits to the verge of the Between World, the place where all souls went at death, there to wait until guided by a Spirit Singer to the Gate of the Upper World. Then, as was the Gift of Spirit Singers, he had gone fully into the Between World himself. Now he was binding their spirits to him, taking minute sparks of their being into his own, sparks that would draw the whole like a lodestone drawing iron when they died. Otherwise, Amarynth knew, the natural ties of spirits to bodies would keep their souls trapped where their bodies lay; and if that were at sea, they would be forced to haunt the empty deep until the End.

Amarynth, too, had the Gift, and many times her grandfather had taken her into the Between World. She had seen the phantom images the Lower World cast into the Between World, had learned the patterns of thought that would allow her to take that precious spark from another living soul and embed it in her own. She knew how to do it—but she wasn't being allowed to.

She clenched her fists unconsciously as she watched her grandfather and the three boys sit in silence. Her Gift cut her off from the ordinary world of people, but despite her earlier dark thoughts, she could not wish she did not have it; it was too rare and wonderful a thing to be able to serve the One as her grandfather did—and as she could, if given the chance. But now her grandfather was shutting her out of that service. And without it—

Suddenly her grandfather's hand tightened on his Emblem, his knuckles whitening. He moaned. Sweat erupted on his furrowed brow and his lips moved silently, as the tear-shaped stone on its golden chain glowed brighter and brighter, until it seemed his whole hand burned with purple fire.

Finally, he gasped, and his eyes snapped open. "Amarynth, quickly!" he cried hoarsely.

Without wondering how he knew she was there, she rushed into the room.

"Bring them out!" he whispered, and then his eyes flickered up behind his lids and he slipped down in his chair, unconscious.

Quickly Amarynth touched each boy on the forehead, exerting the slight mental pressure necessary to return their spirits fully to their bodies. They each gasped in turn, then sat up straighter, blinking and rubbing their eyes.

"The Link is forged," she said formally, standing stiffly before them. "May the One favour your journeys this day."

Their faces registered surprise at seeing her, then concern as they looked past her to her grandfather. "The Spirit Singer..." Davin began.

"Go in peace," said Amarynth, in a tone that forestalled questioning. The youths rose quickly, bowed, and touched their fingers to their hearts, then filed out of the Spirit Chamber. Davin lingered a moment, but this time received no encouragement from Amarynth, who stared at him stonily until he followed the others.

Only then did Amarynth turn and drop to her knees beside her grandfather, taking his wrist, feeling the thin pulse racing beneath her fingers. "Grandfather, what's happening to you?" she whispered. "*What's gone wrong?*"

CHAPTER 2

Within a few minutes of the boys' departure, Amarynth's grandfather woke. He covered her hand with his for a moment, breathing deeply, then struggled upright in the chair.

"Grandfather...?" Amarynth whispered.

"I'm all right—for now," he said. "Amarynth, there is something I must tell you. I'd hoped not to worry you..."

"I can't be any more worried than I am!"

He touched her cheek fondly, then let his hand fall back to the armrest. "You know about my dreams. All of them are the same—something pursues me, something black as night, formless but terrible. It chases me, hunts me, through a grey, empty land. And all the time it calls to me, urging me to join it, to become one with it." He shuddered, eyes closed, his words coming faster and faster. "I refuse, of course I refuse, and I run, but it comes after me, gaining, gaining all the time, reaching for me, almost touching me—and then I wake up." His eyes opened suddenly and locked onto Amarynth's. "But each time it gets a little closer."

Amarynth swallowed. "A nightmare—" she began, but her grandfather cut her off with a shake of his head.

"This morning, as I prepared to forge the Link, I went into the Between World—and *the thing was there.* Somewhere. I couldn't see it, but I could sense it, far off, but coming nearer—coming this way."

"Some kind of monster? In the Between World?" Amarynth stared at her grandfather. "How is that possible?"

"I would have sworn it is not. But I know what I felt. And that was why I would not let you assist with the Linking. I didn't want to risk you."

"But what could happen to me in the Between World?" Amarynth protested. "As long as my body is safe here..."

"When I re-entered the Between World with the boys to forge the Link, I felt the thing's presence again at once," her grandfather went on, as though she had not spoken, as if talking to himself. "It was closer, much closer. It knew I was there—and it wanted me. I could feel it. I had to hurry the Linking and spend far too much energy shielding both myself and the boys, trying to hide us from that...that Beast, for that was how it seemed to me: a huge, devouring creature of evil, seeking prey. I think all that saved us was that we were only on the very fringe of the Between World. The Beast searched deeper, somewhere along the Path."

Amarynth wrapped her arms around herself, feeling a chill despite the fire not a dozen steps away. "What are you going to do now, Grandfather?"

"I must consult my books," he said slowly. "There may be some clue..."

"But what if there isn't?"

"Whether there is or not, the next time I must Sing, I will have to confront the Beast. I'll have no choice." He got to his feet, and for a moment clung to the chair, wavering. "There are one or two scrolls that have always been obscure to me. Perhaps..."

Amarynth stood and took his arm. "But Grandfather, what about my studies? How can I learn if I can't enter the Between World? How will I become a Spirit Singer?"

Her grandfather patted her hand. "You have the Gift, child. You *will* be a Spirit Singer. What else could you be?" Gently he removed her fingers from his arm and smiled through the anxiety and fatigue that clouded his face. "Now, aren't those children I hear? Your class is coming."

Amarynth listened, and hearing high-pitched chatter and laughter, frowned. "I'll send them back."

"You will not! Sitting and worrying about what you cannot change will not help you or me or the village. But what you teach those children is vital. You, young lady, will do your duty." His smile took some of the edge off his words.

A little abashed, she looked down. "Yes, Grandfather."

"Good. Now, I think I'll take some breakfast up to the library..."

As her grandfather went out through the curtained arch into the stairwell, Amarynth turned and slowly went the other way. *What if there* is *no way to deal with this—monster?* she thought. *What if it keeps us—Grandfather—from Singing?*

Then the village will die, she answered herself harshly. The people would not remain in a place without Spirit Singers to guide their dead along the Path through the Between World to the Gate of the Upper World. They would go to where there *were* Singers. If they did not, Covedrift would become a village of ghosts, haunted by unSung spirits, pitiful creatures with no power in the Lower World except to bring fear, even to those whom they had loved.

And what would become of her and her grandfather? Her grandfather's answer to her question about her studies echoed in her mind. Indeed, what else could she be but a Spirit Singer? Her life in the tower was all she had ever known. Her grandfather had travelled far into the mountains, to her home village of Lakevale, somehow knowing she had been born with the Gift, that it had, as was its wont, skipped a generation and emerged in his daughter's child. She often wondered how her parents had felt, giving her up; had they wailed, and protested, and sworn at her grandfather, or had they handed her to him with pride and sadness? Her grandfather's silence about her mother, his daughter, made her think the former more likely. But however it had been, tradition and necessity and the law had left her parents no choice; the Gift was rare and could not be wasted.

And because of that same tradition and necessity and law, she had never had any choice, either; she had never even questioned the course of her life until these last few months, when her isolation from normal society had begun to prey on her more and more, as her grandfather seemed to withdraw because of his dreams. Now she knew why he had acted that way, but it didn't salve her growing loneliness.

She wondered often what her life might have been like had she been born without the Gift. She might well be married by now, even a mother: or perhaps she would be helping her father farm, or blacksmith, or helping raise her younger brothers and sisters, if she had any—she didn't even know that.

Yes, she thought, *and perhaps you would be like the girls your age you see in the village market, giggling and whispering and flirting with the boys, with no knowledge about or interest in anything else. That* certainly didn't appeal to her, either. Her life as an apprentice Spirit Singer had developed in her a thirst for knowledge that she could not imagine being quenched in thoughts of bread and babies; but all her learning would do little for her if she could not Sing.

As for her grandfather, he had been a Spirit Singer all his long life, and was too old to farm or fish; they depended for their living upon the food sent them by the villagers. *If we were not Singers,* she thought, *we might very well starve.*

She did her best to shake off her black mood, or at least hide it, as she crossed the antechamber to the classroom and welcomed the first of the village children. Soon there were a dozen, ranging in age from five to thirteen, seated around the child-sized table, chattering happily. They fell silent as she walked to the podium at the front of the room, to which was attached, with a golden chain, one of her grandfather's two precious copies of *The Master's Path.*

As always Amarynth felt a little tingle of awe as she opened the book, its plain green fish-leather binding belying the riches within. She turned the vellum leaves to the place she had marked from the last lesson and motioned to the child seated nearest. "All right, Mindi," she said, smiling at the little blonde-haired girl. "Let's hear you read the story of the Master's first Singing."

Mindi looked both scared and proud, and hesitantly stood up and came to the front. Amarynth helped her up onto the little step she had built for the smaller children, then moved to one side and gave the girl a reassuring smile.

Mindi began to read in a clear, piping voice. "And so, the Master became very good at leaving behind the Lower World for the Between World; but he still didn't know what he was supposed to do once he got there, though he could feel it was something important.

"Then one day a terrible thing happened. A little boy climbing on the rocks near the Master's house fell, and hit his head, and died. Everyone in the village had heard him scream, and they all came running, including the Master.

"And suddenly, the Master sensed that the boy was still there, close by, not in the little broken body his mother was holding to her so tightly, but in the Between World. He—"

Amarynth let the familiar words flow around her and reassure her troubled mind. She knew the story, of course: how the Master had gone into the grey Between World and felt the longing of the dead boy's spirit for something else, something further on; and how suddenly he had seen, high overhead, a shining light. He had reached out for the boy's spirit, taken it to himself, and then had made that first, awesome step onto the Path.

He did what he had to, she thought. *And because he did, all the hundreds of thousands of lost spirits languishing in the Between World were able to move on, to pass through the Gate into the Upper World and the Light of the One.*

Mindi was still reading, a little softer now. "But as the Master approached the glowing, golden Gate, he had to stop, because the Gate was closed, and he didn't know how to open it..."

Amarynth was startled by how far she had read. "Thank you, Mindi," she said. "You did very well. Jafis, why don't you come up next?"

Though Jafis was an older boy, in his last year in the

tower school, he wasn't as good a reader as Mindi. Sometimes he had to stop and sound out the angular letters, but he was too proud to look to Amarynth for help. Because of that she let him struggle through on his own.

"And as the Master stood there, he rea—realized that behind him was a host of other spirits, wa—waiting in a kind of deep, expe—expec—expectant silence..."

And then came the miracle, Amarynth thought. *The Gate opened. The One Himself welcomed the Master and all the dead who had followed him across the Between World into the Upper World...*

...and then the One sent the Master back.

She shook her head in wonder, as she did every time she thought of it. The Master had entered the Upper World, the Eternal Land, had spoken to the One, the Creator, and then had returned to live out a normal lifespan in the Lower World, where he had sought out the many others who, through the grace of the One, were suddenly being born with the Gift. Trained by the Master, they had become the first Spirit Singers.

And yet, he had left them so little. His teachings were simple: treat others as you wish to be treated. Help those who need help. Live in harmony. Live in peace. His own writings made up only a few pages of the tome out of which Jafis still haltingly read; the rest was a history of the Master's life in that mysterious, far-away land where the people had lived before coming to Haven, written by the first Spirit Singer he had trained.

I wish the Master had told us how to fight monsters in the

Between World, she thought, and her mind turned to her grandfather, upstairs in the library. She let Jafis struggle with the Master's story far too long before calling on the next child.

So, the morning passed; a little earlier than usual she sent the children home, then crossed the great hall to the kitchen, entering just as Marta picked up a tray of food for her grandfather. "I'll take that up to him," Amarynth said quickly, and Marta thanked her and returned to her baking.

Amarynth's grandfather didn't look up as she set the tray on the table beside him, among scattered scrolls and stacked books and next to the half-eaten remains of his breakfast. He was bent low over a faded page, his finger tracing the dim, spidery handwriting of some long-dead sage. She went out without speaking and closed the door behind her.

With her grandfather absorbed in research, Amarynth was at loose ends for the rest of the day. She removed her ceremonial clothes and dressed herself boyishly in leather leggings and a simple blue tunic, then went out and clambered down the steep path to the ocean, the still-rising wind tossing her long, dark hair about her face. At the base of the cliff, she sat on the rocks and watched the sea pound the shore, feeling flecks of spray like lost raindrops on her face and arms, listening to the lonely calls of the sea-karils circling overhead.

As the day grew older, clouds rode in on the wind. By

noon, when Amarynth returned to the tower, the sunny morning was only a memory, and thunder grumbled in the darkness engulfing the far horizon.

The storm broke in full fury early in the afternoon, as Amarynth swept the great hall. Lightning flashed, thunder cracked like the sky breaking open, and rain suddenly pelted the shutters, long-since closed against the wind.

Amarynth left her broom and went into the kitchen and out into the yard, hugging herself for warmth in the cold rain and looking out over the ocean, grey slate streaked with white. She thought of Davin and his companions, who had set sail that morning in sunshine, battling the wind and water out there somewhere, and, shivering, returned to the tower.

Her grandfather emerged late in the day for supper, which he ate in the kitchen with Amarynth, while Marta stood by respectfully. But his thoughts were obviously elsewhere, and though he complimented Marta on the meal before returning to the library, Amarynth doubted he even knew what he'd eaten.

She followed him up the stairs. "Have you learned anything?"

"Maybe, maybe," he said vaguely. "I'm not sure yet. It was such a long time ago..." His voice trailed off and he hurried on down the corridor, leaving Amarynth standing at the head of the stairs.

What *was such a long time ago?* she wondered, and

shaking her head, returned to the kitchen to help Marta clean up.

"Is something wrong?" the village woman asked as she pumped water, almost shouting above the noise of the wind, howling around the tower and rattling the shutters.

"No, why?" Amarynth said, instantly alert. It wouldn't do for rumours to be carried to the village about trouble in the tower.

"The Singer just didn't seem quite himself," said Marta, carrying the wash cauldron to the fireplace.

"He's a bit tired," Amarynth said brightly. "He hasn't been sleeping well." *That* was certainly true.

"Hmmm." Marta gave her a sharp look but asked no more questions.

When Amarynth retired that evening, her grandfather was still in the library, books and scrolls now piled on top of both breakfast and lunch trays, hunched over yet another ancient tome in a pool of yellow candlelight. Rain still lashed the window. "Good night," Amarynth ventured as she passed.

Her only reply was a grunt.

It seemed to her she had barely dozed when she woke suddenly to find her grandfather bending over her, candlestick in one hand, shaking her arm. "Amarynth, get up," he said gravely. "I just felt it."

"Felt what?" She sat up, rubbing her eyes.

"The Link. One of the boys has died."

Amarynth felt a cold hand on her heart. *Which one?* "But that means—"

"I have to Sing him." Her grandfather suddenly looked very old to her, old and weary. "I have to face the Beast."

CHAPTER 3

Needing more time to prepare because of the uncertainty surrounding the Singing, Amarynth's grandfather sent her to tell the boy's family. "It's all part of being a Spirit Singer," he said sadly; and then he told her which boy had died, though she had already guessed in her heart: Davin.

As she made her way down the hill in the stormy darkness, picking her way over rain-slicked rocks, the wind twisting and untwisting the folds of her long grey cape, Amarynth felt numb. She couldn't believe that the boy she had talked to, who had taken such an endearing interest in her, was dead, floating drowned somewhere out in the cold ocean. She remembered winking at him only that morning, and felt cheated, robbed of the chance to make more of what had been budding between them. Now he was gone, and though she knew his spirit still lived in the Between World, that was hardly the same. Whatever might have been between them was lost forever—and with it, whatever hope she had had of her long loneliness ending.

Then came guilt. Davin's parents had lost their only child—what was her loss compared to that? And both Davin and her grandfather still had to face the mysterious creature. How could she feel sorry for herself? *She* did not have to go into the Between World to face some formless horror—and yet the fact she did not only made her feel more guilty, as if she were letting down her grandfather.

He had told her he had discovered a few vague passages in ancient books that might have referred to the Beast, but he still didn't know what it portended, how he could avoid it on the Path to the Gate, or even what would happen if he failed. "I had hoped for days, maybe even weeks before I would have to Sing again," he had told her in her room after waking her, as she donned her ceremonial clothes once more. The deep purple fire of his Emblem reflected in his eyes. "There are still books I haven't had time to look at, and I could have consulted other Singers. Old Penrod over in Leeshore might know something, or Scindar in Rockwatch…"

"Old Penrod died last year," Amarynth reminded him. "And he didn't have an apprentice. Don't you remember? Some of Leeshore's people came here." She placed her own dark Emblem around her neck. "And Rockwatch is a week's journey." Her grandfather had hardly seemed to hear her, and that, too, troubled her now, as she came to the verge of Covedrift. It was unlike her grandfather to be forgetful. His mind had so far been untouched by the years that had begun to take their toll of his body.

She paused where the path from the tower joined the village's one street and took a deep breath, trying to centre her mind, as her grandfather had taught her, to present an image of serenity. "The Spirit Singer must appear caring, yet detached," he had said. "You must seem above the troubles of this life. You've been in the Between World; use your knowledge that there is some-thing beyond the Lower World to distance yourself from its strife. Appear as a calm island, a place of shelter in a sea of grief and pain."

But as Amarynth walked through the mud toward the home of the dead boy's family, her detachment was far less complete than would have met with her grandfather's approval. She hesitated in front of the house, her resolve wavering a little; then smoothed her face once more and knocked slowly three times, the third knock seeming to set off answering thunder in the heavens. The door swung open so quickly that Amarynth knew the boy's father had not been sleeping, and his creased, tanned face, lit by the lantern he carried, paled and sagged as he saw her.

With an effort, Amarynth managed to maintain her expression of warm but impersonal concern, and said, simply, "Davin's spirit has come home. My grandfather is preparing to Sing. He bids you come to the tower."

"Paran? What is it?" A woman with hair as long and black as Amarynth's own, just beginning to grey, appeared behind the man. She gasped as she saw Amarynth and clutched her husband's arm. "No..."

"Will you come?" Amarynth said.

Paran put his arm around his wife's shoulders and she buried her head on his chest. "Yes," he whispered.

Amarynth nodded. "We share your grief," she said formally, then turned and walked slowly away, hearing the door of the cottage close behind her and, a moment later, the woman's hopeless cry.

Like the first trickle through a crumbling dam, that sound weakened something within her, and as she once more ascended the path, tears mingled with the rain on her face.

Yellow light glowed through the front doors of the tower, which stood open despite the weather, the rain creating a small lake through which Amarynth's sandaled feet splashed as she entered. She pushed aside the curtain covering the arch into the Spirit Chamber and went in, shaking the water from her cloak and pushing stringy strands of rain-slicked hair from her eyes.

Her grandfather sat in his chair, his eyes closed and his fingers steepled once more. "His rigging broke," he said as Amarynth entered. "The mainsail went with a run. The boat turned broadside, and a towering sea capsized her. The boom struck Davin on the head." He opened his eyes, then, looked up at her, and smiled faintly. "He is lost, and alone, and very, very young, Amarynth. As young as you."

Amarynth's hand trembled as she hung her cloak on a hook near the door. "His parents are coming."

Her grandfather nodded.

She went to him. "He was their only son. I heard his mother crying like—like an unSung spirit." She put her arm around her grandfather's neck and leaned her head on his shoulder. "You told me to be an island of serenity," she said in a small voice. "But I cried all the way back."

Her grandfather hugged her. "Child, serenity doesn't mean being uncaring. Davin's spirit isn't lost; it's here with us now. And I'm going to lead him to the Upper World. That's where our serenity comes from—from doing what must be done for those who have died. It doesn't mean becoming cold and rigid like ice." He smoothed her hair and smiled at her. "You liked Davin, didn't you?"

Amarynth nodded. "He was the first boy from the village who wasn't too frightened of me to forget I was an apprentice Spirit Singer. I'd hoped..." Her voice trailed off.

"I've cried many times since becoming a Spirit Singer," her grandfather said softly. "I've cried for every family left behind, and for the lonely lives of those who were Sung unmourned. I've cried for the lost souls who are unSung, who haunt the places where they died and bring fear to those left behind. And I've cried for those spirits that I have Sung to the Gate of the Upper World, only to see them cry out in terror when that Gate opens and flee the Light, to wander in the Between World until the End—and those are the saddest of all." He smiled a little. "Though we need have no fear of that with Davin. He is a good lad. His parents will be comforted." Then his smile faded. "And often, Amarynth, I've cried for myself. I've seen too many old friends laid out on the dais." His voice dropped low. "I saw my wife...your grandmother...lying there." He paused, then gently pushed her away and looked into her eyes, brushing a tear from her cheek with his gnarled hand. "There's nothing wrong with crying. Just remember that you're crying for yourself—not for Davin. He's going home."

"But what about the Beast?" Amarynth whispered. "Will it let you pass to the Gate?"

Her grandfather's expression suddenly closed. "It must not hinder Davin. I won't allow it."

"But—"

"Please, Amarynth." Her grandfather gestured to the other chair. "Light the candle, then be seated. Centre yourself."

"You want me to go with you?" Amarynth felt a burst of eagerness mixed with fear.

"No!" he said sharply, then more softly, "No. You may observe the start of the journey, and await my return, from the verge of the Between World, but you are not to follow me—not until I know the nature of this creature. Understood?"

"Yes, Grandfather."

"Good." He closed his eyes once more as Amarynth took a straw from the bundle by the fire, lit the end, and then lit the candle at the head of the dais. It burned with a purple flame, echoing the light of her grandfather's Emblem, and she sat opposite him and gazed at it, this time centring herself far more completely. *Imagine your being, your spirit, condensed to a single intense spark, burning within your body*, she could almost hear her grandfather say. *Focus on that spark. Locate it within you. Make it burn hot and bright, as hot and bright as you can. Always be aware of where that spark is, for that is your guide home from the Between World. Lose it, let it go out, and you could wander forever with the lost souls.*

She was aware, distantly, that Davin's parents had entered, and stood at the foot of the dais, but her attention remained focused inward, and her eyes, too, were now closed. "Your son's spirit is here with us," she heard her grandfather say, and indeed she could see it in her mind, a second spark of light, hovering over her head. Her grandfather was a third spark, more brilliant than her or Davin combined, like a torch lighting the darkness.

Slowly that darkness gave way to formless grey, and then it took on shape. Around her rose the walls of the tower, and she could see Davin's parents, clinging to one another for support, but everything was semi-transparent, like smoked crystal. She could also see the silvery, endless sea, and a shadowy image of Covedrift—and her grandfather, as straight and tall and young in the Between World as Davin, who now stood beside him, looking about with bewilderment. Her grandfather's spirit burned bright as a torch in his chest, and a bright spark flamed near Devin's heart, as well; and Amarynth, looking down, saw her own life aglow in her breast.

"Where am I?" Davin asked, turning to Amarynth's grandfather. "Spirit Singer, what is this place?"

"It is called the Between World," her grandfather replied. "My son, what do you remember?"

"I remember the storm...it came up so suddenly." His voice trailed off. "I was so scared..."

"Fear is nothing to be ashamed of," said Amarynth's grandfather gently. "What else do you remember?"

"I remember...wind. Waves washing over the boat. I could hardly hold her—but there had been no time to reef. I tried to lash the tiller, but the rope broke. Then— then there was an awful tearing sound, and I saw the halyard snap. I lunged at it, but it flew from my hand. A wave hit me, and I lost my grip on the tiller, and then the mainsail came crashing down and the boom..." He touched his head. "The pain..." He looked at Amarynth's grandfather. "I'm dead, aren't I?" he said wonderingly.

"Yes, child."

"And they..." He looked at his parents. "Oh, my poor parents...can't I talk to them, tell them how much I love them?"

"We will tell them," said Amarynth's grandfather. "If you made your presence known to them, you would only terrify them. You don't belong in that world any longer, my son."

"I belong in this one?" He stared around into the greyness. "I don't like what I see of it..."

"No; here you are only passing through." Amarynth's grandfather took Davin's hand and looked skyward, and suddenly a swirling, shimmering light appeared above their heads and, stretching up into it at an impossible angle, a silvery path, soaring up and up. Amarynth gazed along it to its farthest reaches, searching for some sign of the creature her grandfather had sensed—and wondering what else lay along it. Someday she would make that journey alone, and, if she completed it, stand before the Gate to the Upper World—and then her Emblem would light, and she would be able to lead others through the Between World and open the Gate for them, and would be a true Spirit Singer at last.

"Our path lies that way," said her grandfather, pointing up along the silvery trail. "Shall we go?"

Davin looked at Amarynth, almost shyly. "Are you coming, too?"

She shook her head.

"Oh." He smiled at her. "I wish—I wish we'd had more time together."

The spark of Amarynth's spirit flickered a little. "So do I," she said softly.

"We must go, Davin," said her grandfather.

Davin looked at his parents once more, but already as if they were people he once knew fondly, but many years before. "I'm ready."

"The Singing begins," Amarynth's grandfather said,

his voice echoing eerily in her ears, for her body in the Lower World heard it even as her mind did in the Between World, and she knew he had spoken out loud for the benefit of Davin's parents. Then she heard him start to sing, as she had so many times before, a simple series of four notes, turned over and over about themselves; and in the blink of an eye, he and Davin stood on the Path high overhead, standing impossibly at right angles to the shadowy plain below.

Amarynth's grandfather looked down at her. "Watch," was all he said, then he and Davin were gone, dwindling along the Path as fast as thought.

"Goodbye, Davin," she whispered.

Time was meaningless in the Between World. Amarynth stood and gazed upward for what might have been ten seconds or ten hours. Then, suddenly, her grandfather was with her again—and her spirit wavered.

The body he wore in the Between World was no longer young and hale but older than his body in the Lower World, shrivelled, almost skeletal. "Back to the Lower World!" he cried to Amarynth, eyes wide with horror. "It comes!"

And then Amarynth looked beyond him, up the Path, and saw, rushing down toward her, an amorphous black shape, a nothingness that swallowed the Path's silvery glint as it came. She gaped at it, frozen with terror, until her grandfather shouted, "Flee!" and seemed to reach inside her, touching the spark of her spirit.

The grey of the Between World shattered around her

like crystal smashed against a wall; then her eyes snapped open and she was in the Lower World, heart pounding, cold sweat beading her face. She lurched upright and scrambled across the dais on her hands and knees to her grandfather, but even as she reached for him he cried out and stiffened—and the light of his Emblem flared and died.

"Grandfather!" Amarynth screamed. She seized his shoulders, shaking him; but his eyes remained closed and the stone that hung about his neck remained as black as her own.

She turned stricken eyes to Davin's parents, who were staring at her. "The Spirit Singer is dead!" she choked out.

Davin's mother gasped, and his father stepped forward, white-faced, fists clenched. "*What about my son?*"

But Amarynth, holding her grandfather's lifeless body, staring through tear-filled eyes at the flames leaping in the hearth, hardly heard him.

CHAPTER 4

In the grey light of early morning, Amarynth stood in the kitchen doorway and looked out over the sea. The rain had settled to a steady drizzle but showed no sign of stopping. Water spouted from a drainpipe into the kitchen yard, then ran down a gully to the cliff, where it sprang into empty space and plunged to the rocks below.

The wind had dropped, smoothing the waves that had killed Davin, and far out over the water Amarynth saw two black specks—the returning boats of the other First Sailors.

They're returning, but my grandfather isn't, Amarynth thought, and quickly closed her eyes and repeated a calming exercise. Very soon, she knew, the village elders would arrive, and though the tale of her sorrow at her grandfather's death would have been told by Davin's parents, open grief from a Spirit Singer was unseemly. "An island of calm," she reminded herself, but the words only reminded her more strongly of her grandfather, and her eyes filled again as she went back into the kitchen.

Marta had not yet come from the village, and Amarynth was uncertain she would, knowing the Spirit Singer lay dead in the tower. But Amarynth felt no desire for breakfast anyway, and crossed through the storeroom into the stairwell, then pushed through the curtained archway into the Spirit Chamber once more.

Her grandfather lay on the dais as Amarynth had seen so many others lie, sometimes horribly wounded, but often as though they were merely asleep. Thus did her grandfather appear, but Amarynth knew his spirit had left forever, that the bright flame of his soul could never again return to his body.

She remembered those last terrifying seconds in the Between World, when the formless horror bore down on her and her grandfather forced her back into the Lower World, and her composure wavered again. "Grandfather, where are you?" she whispered.

Spirit Singers made their own journeys to the Gate; they were not Sung. But she had seen the Path swallowed by the Beast. Had her grandfather found his way to the Upper World? Or did he wander the Between World, lost? That prospect alone was enough to make Amarynth feel sick, but there was a worse possibility that she hardly dared consider—that the Beast had somehow taken him, devoured him...destroyed him.

And what about Davin? His father's question of the night before burned in her mind, but she still had no answer. After the boy's grieving parents had left the tower she had almost re-entered the Between World to search for him and her grandfather, but her fear of the Beast was too great, the memory of its horror too fresh.

Now she wondered miserably if she had failed them both. Perhaps if she had gone back to the Between World at once she could have done something, anything. She would never know, unless sometime as a full-fledged Singer she found their spirits wandering...

A full-fledged Singer? she thought. *When will that be, with no one to teach you? And can you ever bring yourself to return to the Between World, knowing that thing lurks there?*

For a moment she wished more strongly than ever before that she had not been born with the Gift, that she had lived out her life in Lakevale with the parents she had no memory of, unaware of what lay beyond death.

Someone knocked on the tower's front doors, which she had closed and barred after Davin's parents left. She straightened, repeated her calming exercise, then entered the antechamber, lifted the big wooden bar, and swung the doors inward.

Three men bowed and touched their chests, then came in, water streaming from their grey cloaks as they stamped mud from their boots. "Elder Caison, Elder Eklar, Elder Achan," Amarynth greeted them gravely. Despite their titles, they were only middle-aged, at least twenty years younger than her grandfather—though still thirty years older than she. Chosen by the villagers, they were all steady, thoughtful men, "one eye on the rigging and the other on the horizon," as the saying went. Now Amarynth read the concern in their eyes, but they did not start with questions, instead following her silently into the Spirit Chamber and kneeling by her grandfather while she stood by the lighted candle at his head.

Caison, the usual spokesman, stood first. "We share your grief," he said.

Amarynth inclined her head calmly, though the warmth and compassion she heard in his voice threatened to melt her composure from the inside.

"I must ask you," he went on, "if Covedrift now has a Spirit Singer."

Amarynth knew the implications of the question; if she could not carry out her grandfather's duties, another Spirit Singer would have to be found. Otherwise the village would dwindle, as Leeshore had when Penrod died.

"I am a Spirit Singer," she replied carefully. "But I am yet only an apprentice."

"Then we must look elsewhere," said Caison heavily.

Silently, she nodded assent.

"It is as I said," said Eklar, the youngest of the three. "We must seek out the wandering Spirit Singers those mountain traders told us of a month ago."

"The traders did not seem easy with them," pointed out Achan. "They were very pleased to learn that our Spirit Singer had been here more than fifty years. You remember they said they would mark our village on their maps and return should any of their number die on their journey to the north."

"These wandering Singers are something new and unknown, it's true," said Eklar. "But what choice do we have? Scindar in Rockwatch is a week's journey away, and none of us can afford to lose two weeks of fishing to fetch him and return. We'd starve, come winter."

"Eklar is right," said Caison. "We must send someone to bring one of these wandering Singers from the mountains to Covedrift." He looked at Amarynth. "He need only complete Amarynth's training, then he can be on his way."

Amarynth nodded and smiled slightly, but inside she was in turmoil. *Wandering Singers? How is that possible?* Her grandfather had told her it took days for a Singer to establish a Path, and it was terrible work, physically and mentally draining. A Singer could enter the Between World from anywhere, and he could use another Singer's Path, but if he tried to Sing without a Path both he and the spirit he Sang would be lost.

"But who shall we send?" Achan queried. "As you say, none of us can afford to leave now."

Amarynth took a deep breath, and said, "Elders, if you please." They turned to her. "There is only one person who can and should make the journey—me."

"But you're only a girl," protested Achan. "You can't wander the wild country on your own—"

"I am a Spirit Singer," said Amarynth sharply. "Only an apprentice, it's true—but still a Singer, and recognizable as such." She touched her Emblem. "No one in all Haven will harm me."

"Amarynth—" began Caison, but she shook her head.

"No, Elder Caison. I have decided to go, and you know you have no authority to forbid me. I promise I will return with a Spirit Singer for Covedrift." She glanced at her grandfather. "It is my duty."

The elders looked at one another, then bowed and saluted her. "As you wish," said Caison. "If we may assist in any way..."

"There is one thing," said Amarynth, and swallowed.

"Yes?"

"I need help...to bury my grandfather."

"Of course," Caison said gently. "But first, let the people come up and pay their respects. They are waiting below." He looked down at the old man. "Your grandfather was well-loved."

Amarynth could only nod, no longer trusting herself to speak, wishing they would leave before she disgraced herself again with open grief. Perhaps sensing her distress, Caison touched the others on their shoulders and the three of them went out. As the Spirit Chamber's curtain swept closed behind them, Amarynth sat down hard in the chair next to her grandfather's body and rested her head in her hands, drawing long, shuddering breaths.

She had just promised to bring back a Spirit Singer, and she would—but would *any* Spirit Singer be able to deal with the Beast? Or would that Singer, too, die as her grandfather had?

If there truly are wandering Spirit Singers, they must be very powerful, she thought. *Maybe they'll know what to do.*

All the rest of the day, mourners climbed from the village to the tower, some standing silent beside her grandfather's body, others weeping gently, rocking in place. Outside, four young fishermen dug a grave at the foot of the garden, near the cliff. As the sun neared the horizon, the young men, with the Elders and Amarynth pacing silently beside them, carried the shrouded body of Amarynth's grandfather to the grave, laid him in it, and then filled it with earth and covered it with heaped, grey rocks. After a moment of silence, the elders and the young men made their way back to the village, leaving Amarynth alone. She stayed by the grave until it grew dark, then made her lonely way to the empty tower, to cry herself asleep in its silence and solitude.

The next morning, Caison led a strong young therra mare, the colour of milk, to the tower, and helped Amarynth load the beast with food, water, clothing, and bedding. He bid her a grave farewell, then left her. She went back into the tower to put more supplies into a backpack and retrieve her grandfather's favourite stout walking stick, carved of silvery driftwood. When she emerged, she fed the therra a bit of carra leaf she had found in the kitchen, patting its velvety nose while it chewed contentedly. When it was done, it rumbled in its throat and butted its long, narrow head against her side, and she laughed a little.

But the laughter died as she looked back at the forlorn cairn of stones, marking her grandfather's grave. *His body's there*, she thought, *but where is his spirit?* And then she looked beyond the grave to the ocean and wondered the same thing about Davin.

Those will be my first questions for these wandering Singers, she told herself.

With an almost physical wrench, she turned away from the only home she had ever known and started toward the distant, saw-toothed blue ridge that marked the inland horizon.

CHAPTER 5

In a pouch at the belt of her new white tunic, Amarynth carried a map of northern Haven, showing clearly the route she must follow to the nearest of the mountain villages, Cragshadow. The way led across a pleasant green plain that sloped gradually up from sea to soaring peaks. Dotted with trees and myriad small lakes, but uninhabited, it brought to Amarynth's mind the tales of the First Landing, when those who had fled across the ocean from the Old Land had first looked upon Haven, their new home.

No one living knew what had brought about that dreadful journey across the deep, a journey that took a hundred days and far more than a hundred lives, as ship after ship foundered in terrible storms. The First Landers had never told their children or written in any history why they had fled—though the tale of the voyage itself was well-known—and the knowledge had died with them.

Now, after more than two centuries, people had spread across Haven, as far north and farther than Covedrift. But only fisherman had come to the most remote regions, and they had come by ship, so there were still vast tracts of wilderness inland, such as the one across which Amarynth now made her way, the sun warming her neck, her legs finding an easy rhythm of walking despite the urgency and uncertainty of her quest. With the dreadful moment of departure behind her, she felt almost as if she had been released from a cage, the cage in which her Gift had forced her to live all her life.

I tried *to break out of it,* she thought as she took off her boots and splashed barefoot through a swift-running creek, the water darkening the bottoms of her sky-blue leggings. *I really did. But everyone in the village treated me like I was my grandfather—bowing and saluting and never talking unless I spoke to them or until I was gone.* She paused in the middle of the stream to refill her leather water pouch, and the therra took the opportunity to refill itself. It drank and drank and drank while her feet slowly went numb, until finally she gave a sharp tug on the reins, earning herself a reproachful look, and led the beast onto the far bank. As she put on her boots again she squinted at the sun, setting just about where Covedrift had to be. Now she was on her own, and should she meet anyone, they would see her, and not her grandfather's granddaughter. The idea appealed to her, though it made her feel slightly guilty, as though she were being untrue to his memory.

I wonder if he *ever felt caged by his Gift?* she thought suddenly, and wished she had asked him. She had always felt she couldn't talk to him about her frustration and loneliness—but she had never tried. *Maybe I should have.*

After a night beneath the stars, lullabied by the sighing of the wind through the branches of a nearby copse of trees, Amarynth arose stiffly and limped on her way once more, wondering ruefully how the easy stride that had seemed to come so naturally the day before could have become so painful in just a few hours, and envying the supple movements of the therra, who obviously had never heard of such a thing as sore muscles.

However, as day followed day she toughened and regained her pleasure in walking. Her pleasure in the beautiful country through which she passed never waned. The weather continued to smile on her, and she let her quest and the horrors that had precipitated it slip to the back of her mind. In the bright sunshine it was hard to believe in evil creatures lurking in the Between World.

It was hard to believe that her grandfather was dead.

The character of the country changed as she began to climb, the lush green grass of the lower plain giving way to tough, scraggly weeds, the broad, shady trees replaced by darker, spikier ones. At last, she topped a ridge and saw only forest ahead of her, mounting to the sky on ever-higher slopes, and realized she was on the threshold of the mountains.

She dug into her pouch for the map and held it up to catch the long orange rays of the sun, setting behind her. Cragshadow was marked by the up-thrust bit of granite, sharp as a spear, that gave it its name, and the fiery light illuminated it perfectly off to her right, no more than six or seven miles away.

"Come on, lad, not much further," she said to the therra, and started down the ridge into the forest.

At first she caught frequent glimpses of the Crag above the trees, but as the sky deepened to indigo, and then to the glittering blackness of full night, she began to hesitate and turn one way and the other. Finally, she stopped and admitted to the therra she no longer knew in which direction to travel. "Looks like we'll have to wait one more night," she told it.

She tied it to a handy bush, then dragged its load from its back and dropped the packs to the ground, laughing as the animal rumbled with pleasure and stretched, the muscles in its sleek black neck standing out like cords of wood even in the thin light of the stars. "I'll light a fire," she said.

A few minutes later leaping flames warded off the chill wafting down from the high peaks. The flickering red light danced on the rough grey trunks of the surrounding trees, casting wavering shadows like strange creatures moving about just on the edge of sight. At first Amarynth hardly noticed, as she boiled water and made mithrin tea, the sweet, clean smell of the herb wafting over her like a balm; but when she had drunk the tea, and toasted and eaten her bread and cheese, she became uneasily aware of that dark dance, which brought back to her full-force what she had seen in the Between World. If the sunshine had banished black thoughts, the forest night brought them back redoubled, and Amarynth shuddered. *There'll be a Spirit Singer in Cragshadow*, she thought, and, closing her eyes to shut out the disquieting darkness, curled up in her blankets, willing herself to sleep and the night to end.

Some hours later she jerked awake. The fire had died to a bed of embers, barely aglow. A rising wind whistled through the trees. The therra snorted and pulled at its lead. Amarynth went to it, patting it comfortingly on the neck while staring around at the chill darkness. "You woke me up, silly," she whispered to it, but in her heart she felt it had been something else—some sound that did not belong in the forest.

Five minutes passed, and she felt her eyelids growing heavy. With a final pat for the therra, she returned to her cooling blankets and burrowed into them again. For a moment longer she listened wide-eyed, then sleep took her.

The next time she awoke it was to the high-pitched scream of the therra and the iron grip of an armoured hand on her right arm. The hand hauled her upright and, in the yellow light of a torch held somewhere nearby, pulled her close to a black steel helm. Eyes glinted behind two narrow slits; then, as suddenly as though she had become too hot to hold, the man released her. She staggered back, staring frantically around, breath rasping in her ears. Three more of the silent, black-armoured figures surrounded her; one behind her held the torch, another gripped the therra's lead, and the third carried her pack and the beast's saddlebags.

The one who had pulled her from her bed pointed at her chest, and she looked down at her Emblem, reflecting sparks of torchlight. The other three formed a cordon around her and started forcing her through the forest, the therra trotting as far behind the man who held its lead as possible, as though afraid to come in contact with him.

Still only minutes out of sleep, Amarynth wondered for a moment if this were all some bizarre dream, from which she would wake in a moment. Who were these silent men, dressed all in black and fully armoured— armoured against what, in these sparsely inhabited lands? Amarynth had seen drawings in her grandfather's books of the warriors who had been among the First Landers, but he had told her the only men still trained in arms were those who patrolled the streets of the distant city of Havenheart.

Yet here, not ten days' journey from Covedrift, were four men who might have stepped from the pages of those history books—except the First Landers never wore black.

As the night air revived her, Amarynth became more and more frightened—and angry. "I am a Spirit Singer," she announced suddenly, in her best authoritative voice.

"You have no right to force me somewhere against my will."

The men didn't even look at her, and never slackened their pace.

She stopped walking, but the warriors simply seized her arms and dragged her, bare toes scraping over dirt and roots of trees, and she quickly regained her feet. *If I were a full Spirit Singer they would never dare...*she thought, then seemed to hear her grandfather telling her that a true Spirit Singer realized his Gift was just that and did not make him better than anyone else. "I have known arrogant Spirit Singers," he told her. "Such arrogance never lasts. If they are not brought low in this world by people who turn against them, they are brought low in the Between World at the Gate."

An island of serenity, Amarynth thought, and as they continued their steady march through the forest, the sky just beginning to grey with pre-dawn light, she repeated calming exercises over and over. She was a Spirit Singer; she would not bluster or threaten. No doubt the commander of these mute warriors would deal with her better.

The sky was high and blue, though the morning sun had yet to clear the peaks, when she and her captors emerged suddenly from the woods into the village street of Cragshadow. It was a tiny settlement, even smaller than Covedrift, one where each family eked out an existence from small gardens, hunting, and shepherding. Already there were people in the street, but as Amarynth and the warriors strode past, they pressed their backs against their two-story, peak-roofed houses and looked away. Amarynth gazed into each face, but no one met her eyes until, as she and her escorts neared the largest building in the village, a long, narrow structure with a tall red roof, a young man sitting on his porch step, head in his hands, glanced up, then leaped to his feet, staring at the Emblem around her neck. Then she was past him, the warriors forcing her up the path to the large building.

Opening the door, they thrust her inside. For a moment she was blind in the darkness, but gradually she made out a long, empty room, the roof supported by four wooden pillars carved with shapes of men and animals. The centre of the floor held a round, blackened pit, and high overhead the wind whispered across a smoke hole, through which Amarynth could see a tiny circle of blue sky.

Only two of her captors had entered with her. One stopped by the door and dropped her packs and, she noted indignantly, her boots. *They could have at least let me put those on before marching me through the forest*, she thought angrily. The other pushed her to the nearest pillar, forced her to sit down against it, then pulled her arms back around it and bound her to it with a thong of leather around her wrists. Then, without a backward glance, both men went out, leaving her immobile and furious, calmness and serenity forgotten.

Time passed. Amarynth began to feel hungry...and puzzled. Surely they didn't intend to just leave her there until she starved. They must have gone to tell someone of her capture. But who? And when would they be back? She shook her head. *There can't be a Spirit Singer in this village. He would never allow—*

She heard a faint sound, and suddenly the door swung open and the young man she had seen on the porch earlier dashed in, a wicked-looking dagger in his hand. He ran over to her and she gasped and shrank away, but he whispered, "I've come to free you. The Black Guards have gone to the next village for a Wanderer; they won't be back until tomorrow morning."

"But didn't they post a—" Amarynth started to whisper; then saw the blood on the young man's knife and swallowed her words.

Her rescuer didn't answer; he cut her bonds, wiped the knife quickly on his pant leg, then sheathed it. As he pulled her to her feet she resisted. "Who are you? What's going on?"

His answer was almost angry. "You're a Spirit Singer, aren't you?"

"Yes, but—"

"My daughter is dead. You have to Sing her." And with that he seized her hand and pulled her toward the door, and she, dumb with shock, followed unprotestingly.

CHAPTER 6

Outside, in the sunshine, Amarynth's rescuer turned away from the street and started up a narrow, steep trail that began between two mighty trees, whose trunks leaned apart as though they had once been a single plant that had been split by lightning. Up toward the granite crag looming over the village they climbed, and every few feet they passed some small memorial; a cairn of black rock, a lovingly tended flowering shrub, a statue, a youth's likeness painted on a square of wood. Amarynth would have liked to look more closely at them, but her rescuer pulled her insistently upward.

The higher they went the fewer of the memorials there were, until at last they came out of the forest at the base of a towering cliff—and there, sheltered beneath an overhang of the rock, was a small wooden cottage with a slate roof, a trickle of smoke rising from its stone chimney.

The young man's hand on Amarynth's wrist tightened, and he muttered something as he led her to the house. He threw open the polished door and shouted, "The chimney is smoking! Do you want to bring more Black Guards?"

Amarynth heard a gasp from the dim-lit interior, then saw someone outlined for a moment against a small fire in the hearth before the burning wood was scattered. The young man pulled her inside and closed the door behind her, and she blinked in the semi-darkness, waiting for her eyes to adjust, breathing hard from the climb.

Gradually she made out more details of the hut. There was only one room, warmed by the now-dying fire. A little light crept in around the closed and bolted shutters, but most of the illumination came from a single candle on a simple wooden table near the hearth. There was also a cot, a few simple clothes hung on a row of hooks over the bed, and, on a rough-made cabinet, a clay pitcher and a wooden bowl filled with water.

At the table sat a young woman, only a few years older than Amarynth, her pale hands twisting. Tears streaked her face, pale in the candlelight, and her lip trembled as she met Amarynth's gaze.

Before her on the table lay a bundle, no more than two feet long, wrapped in white cloth and wound round with a plaid scarf. Amarynth looked from the woman to the bundle, and her heart leaped suddenly as she realized what it must be.

The young man went to his wife and kissed her on

the cheek. "I'm sorry, my love; I shouldn't have shouted at you."

His wife nodded without speaking, her eyes on Amarynth; and Amarynth read there a hope that went through her like a knife. *I can't!* she cried inwardly. *But how can I tell them...?*

"My name is Potras," said the young man. "This is my wife, Elessa. And this..." He indicated the long white bundle, and his voice broke. "This is our daughter, Timara." He paused, then went on harshly, "Things have been bad since the Black Guards came. They took our flocks, our stores of grain—they left us almost nothing. Timara grew sick—there was nothing to feed her. She fell asleep two nights ago...and never woke up."

Timara? Amarynth thought, reaching out with her mind—and at once sensed the child's spirit and, even without entering the Between World, her fear and loneliness.

"You must help us," Potras said, his voice like a too-tight viol string. "You must. Timara must be Sung...soon. Before the Black Guards find out she is dead. Before they bring a Wanderer."

"I don't understand," Amarynth said. "Doesn't Cragshadow have a Spirit Singer?"

"No longer." For the first time Elessa spoke, her tone bitter. "The Black Guards took more than our grain and our animals."

Amarynth stared, shocked. "They took your Spirit Singer?"

Potras nodded. "Talus was a young man—a strong man. He fought them. But you have seen them...what can one man do?"

"But surely the villagers—?"

"Cowards," Elessa cried. "All cowards. They did nothing. Not one lifted a hand to help him!"

"I was in the forest, hunting, or I would have," said Potras angrily. "Together Talus and I could have given a good account of ourselves. But when I returned, he was already gone."

"But the village can't survive without a Spirit Singer!" Amarynth protested.

"Oh, we have one," said Potras sarcastically. "One of the new ones. A Wanderer."

The rumours the Elders heard, Amarynth thought sickly. *Wandering Spirit Singers*. She had known it was wrong— unnatural. But she had never thought... "This Wanderer has the Gift?"

"So he says. But he wears black instead of white. And he has no permanent dwelling—people don't bring him their dead, he goes to them, right into their homes. And his ritual—I have seen Talus Sing more than once. I watched him send my parents to the Upper World, and a friend who died in a rockslide. Always we brought the dead to him. Always his ritual was one of peace. There was a calmness, a caring about him—you knew he understood your grief, but that he could also see beyond it, to something better..." Potras broke off. "There's none of that with the Wanderer. It's as if—as if he *enjoys* people's grief, as if he finds *pleasure* in Singing the dead."

He fixed Amarynth with steely eyes. "I will not deliver my daughter into such a one's hands. But I will have no choice if the Black Guards learn she is dead and tell the Wanderer. I had thought to flee—but Elessa is not strong. She can't travel or live in caves or forest shelters. And where would we go? The Black Guards and the Wanderers are all through the mountains. All the true Spirit Singers have fled or been taken." His eyes dropped to her Emblem, then flicked back to her face. "But then I saw you brought into the village."

Amarynth clutched the dark stone, hiding it. "But I'm only an apprentice!"

"Better than a Wanderer! At least you know the true Path."

"I can't!" Amarynth cried. "Spirit Singing requires a prepared place. It can't be done just anywhere. And I don't have the knowledge or the power to—"

"This *is* a prepared place," Potras said forcibly. "This is Talus's Place of Singing. Here the dead have always been brought."

Amarynth stared around, contrasting the simplicity of the hut with the austere massiveness of her grandfather's tower. Unconsciously she had thought all Singers would live in similar circumstances—yet there was no reason the Path could not be found here as well as anywhere else.

She swallowed. *You were due to make your lone trip on the Path*, she told herself. *You know what must be done.*

But to take the child's spirit with her...it was never done, not the first time. Sometimes Singers failed in their lone journeys, turned back without ever reaching the Gate. What would happen to Timara then? And the Beast was out there somewhere. What would become of the child—and herself!—if that dark creature came upon them?

You're a Spirit Singer—it's your duty, the other part of her replied implacably.

Echoing her thoughts, Potras said, "You're a Spirit Singer. You must help us. You're all we have!"

"Please," whispered Elessa, one pale hand resting on the bundle before her.

Amarynth met her eyes—and made up her mind. "All right." She released her Emblem and let it swing freely, glittering slightly with reflected candle flame. "Even if I lose her, she will at least be safe from the Wanderer. I'll do it."

"Thank you!" breathed Elessa.

"How can I help?" Potras said, and she could hear the relief in his voice. She just hoped it wasn't premature.

"Keep watch. That's all. I must not be disturbed." Amarynth sat down in the empty chair across from Elessa. She reached out and pulled the candle closer to her, so that its flame filled her vision. Then she drew a deep breath and concentrated on that leaping light, centring herself as she had the day her grandfather died.

It took longer than it had then, for the surroundings were strange and her heart pounded in her ears, but at last she was ready, and stepped into the Between World.

At once she saw Timara, hovering over the ghostly image of the sad bundle on the table, and the child's crying, thin and reedy, filled her mind. She reached out phantasmal arms and drew the little girl to her, rocking her gently and murmuring to her. When at last Timara had quieted, she looked more closely at her surroundings.

The mountains had no substance here; the shadowy hut, its walls transparent, stood on the same endless grey plain from which her grandfather's tower had risen in Covedrift. But above her rose the Path, just as before, disappearing into the vast nothingness that overarched the Between World.

Amarynth started to Sing, the repetition of the simple, ancient musical phrase blotting out the Lower World and, through her Gift, propelling her onto the Path. Suddenly the Between World was no longer a plain, but an infinite grey wall extending above and below her, and then, with frightening speed, dwindling beneath her, vanishing into darkness until she seemed to skim an endless ribbon of glimmering silver like frozen starlight.

But slowly the emptiness around her filled with cloudy shapes that gradually solidified, until she again moved through a vast landscape, not the grey plain of the Between World's border but a place of lush green grass and spreading trees and half-glimpsed thatch-roofed villages huddled among golden fields of grain. The Path took on the appearance of a cart-track, and the sun beat down from the high blue sky until Amarynth began to feel thirsty, hungry, and footsore. The effortless flight of thought became a racking, weary plod, step after step. The ghostly Between World had become all too real, and as the sun inched across the sky, Amarynth found herself wondering for a moment who she was, and why she was driving herself down this endless track. She slowed, almost stopped, then seemed to hear a distant voice telling her she had to keep moving, and limped on, staring down at the sleeping baby in her arms and wondering whose it was.

A young man appeared by the side of the road, lithe and lean and tanned by the sun, naked but for a short linen kilt. He had a scythe slung over one shoulder and was drawing water from a stone well. He upended the bucket over his head, sending the liquid cascading down his bare chest and back. He cocked a friendly eye at Amarynth as she came up, and said, "And what's a pretty lass like you doing, walking this dusty road in the heat of the day? Stop for a minute and I'll give you a drink."

Keep moving, Amarynth seemed to hear. She licked her dry lips and said, "No, thank you."

The young man shook the water from his head as she passed him, spraying her with delicious cool drops. She stumbled, almost turned back—then for a moment saw the sun-drenched fields around her as formless grey mist, and the young man as a beckoning, leering ghost, and gasped and ran, hearing his voice shouting after her, "I can give you a taste of something even sweeter than water, my lass..."

Amarynth closed her eyes, reaching inside for the spark of her soul that had almost gone out, focusing it again. When she looked up the sunlit fields were gone, and she was once more speeding through nothingness.

"The Test," she murmured to herself and to the baby. "Grandfather told me about it. Every time, he said, there's a test—and every time it's different. The lost souls...they want others to be like them, to share their endless exile. Like that boy by the well..." She shuddered. If she had left the Path, she might have become like him, wandering forever in a grey world, her body stiffening and dying in Talus's hut.

Now she looked ahead for the Gate. Her grandfather had always said there was only one Test...

Lightning split the night.

She stared around, shocked. Now she was climbing the Crag, wind screaming around her and thunder crashing against the rocks. Sleet pelted from the heaving black cloud overhead, and the granite glowed a livid green.

And then she saw her grandfather.

He was bound to a stone pillar atop a boulder well off the path, the tattered remnants of his ceremonial robes flapping in the vicious wind. He raised his head, and her feet almost stuttered to a stop when she saw the empty black pits where his eyes had been. "Amarynth? Amarynth, is that you?" he cried above the storm-howl.

Don't answer, she told herself in horror. *It's a Test, another Test, a trick of the Lost Ones...*

"Amarynth, why are you here?" her grandfather shouted. "You're no Spirit Singer! The Beast is waiting for you, Amarynth—waiting for you like it waited for me. It won't let you pass!"

Still Amarynth pressed forward, averting her eyes from the image of her tortured grandfather. But she could not shut out his voice.

"You could have saved me!" he screamed. "You could have helped me escape. Did you want to be the only Spirit Singer in Covedrift? *Is that why you let me die?*" And then, most terribly of all, "*I thought you loved me!*"

Amarynth stopped without thinking, turning toward him. "I did love you, Grandfather!" she cried. "I still do!"

But he had vanished, and Amarynth, motionless on the Path, gaped around at the nothingness. An immense silence surrounded her, a silence broken suddenly by a vibration beneath her feet.

Slowly she turned. Distantly, somewhere on the infinite horizon, she thought she saw a gleam of golden light, a glow that touched her heart like a chord of unutterably sweet music. But an instant later it vanished, hidden behind a formless black mass that rose higher and higher, swallowing the Path—and then suddenly rushed toward her like an unstoppable wave.

The Beast!

In simple, elemental terror, Amarynth turned and fled. Timara woke and screamed in her arms, but she ignored the infant spirit, feeling a growing rumble beneath her feet, and a cold, cold breath, like a wind from the northern wastes, sapping her strength, slowing her steps, numbing her body—

Body? she thought. *I have no body.*

She cast aside the illusion of flesh and sped back along the Path like a shooting star, the flame of her spirit linked intangibly with the tiny spark that was Timara.

Still the Beast pursued, and still it gained, until Amarynth could feel it looming behind her like the Crag itself, ready to fall and—

And what? a part of her thought to ask. *What does it want with me?*

Terror needed no answer. It gave her one last burst of speed, kept her just ahead of the pursuing nightmare, until the border of the Between World rose up before her, and she could see the shadowy shape of Talus's hut.

With all the energy she could muster, she threw aside Timara's spirit, casting it off the Path, safely away from the Beast. And then she crashed into the border and her body, feeling vast rage as the Beast reached for her, an immense icy chill as its limbs passed through where she had been—and then pain.

She gasped the air she had not been breathing, feeling it like fire in her lungs, and reeled upright, head spinning, seizing the table to keep from falling. She stared around. The day had jumped forward to the edge of night, and Elessa and Peter sat by the cold hearth, leaning on each other as though exhausted. But when

Elessa looked up and met Amarynth's gaze, she clutched her husband's arm, and he leaped up. "Is it done?"

She could not tell them the truth—she didn't even know what it was. "It is done," she said, and then couldn't look at them as they embraced, Elessa crying again and, this time, Potras weeping with her, great, body-wracking sobs, as though only now could he grieve for the daughter he had lost.

Amarynth touched the still-dark form of her Emblem, tasting bitter defeat—and heard, as if from a great distance, the heartbroken cry of an abandoned child. *Timara*, she thought. *I released her from her body, but I didn't Sing her to the Gate. She has only one thing to cling to—me.*

Amarynth heard that cry again. Until she was able to finish what she had begun, she always would.

And then she heard another sound, nearer and far more tangible—a harsh fanfare of trumpets.

Potras jerked upright. "The Wanderer!" he gasped, and Amarynth seemed to feel once more the bitter breath of the Beast.

"You must flee!" Elessa cried, scrambling to her feet. "Potras, we can't be found with her!"

"The Cragway," Potras said.

Elessa's eyes widened. "No!"

"What is the Cragway?" Amarynth demanded, feeling her own urgency. She had met the Black Guards; she had no desire to meet their master.

"A path. Steep and dangerous—but secret. Talus used it to come and go without being seen. If only he had used it that last day..."

"But Talus was raised in the mountains," Elessa protested. "The Spirit Singer..."

"Has climbed on sea-cliffs all her life," Amarynth put in. "The Cragway sounds perfect." *But where do I go after that?* she wondered, then firmly put the thought from her mind. One thing at a time—and escape came first.

"Once they discover you're missing, every Black

Guard in the mountains will be searching for you," Potras said grimly. He snuffed out the candle. "Come."

Amarynth gathered her pack and followed him and Elessa into the gathering night. Thunder grumbled somewhere in the mountains, and Amarynth, looking up, could see no stars or glow of sunlight; the peaks were smothered in cloud. A chill wind blew down from the heights, and as Potras led her along the base of the Crag, Amarynth opened her pack and drew out a fine woollen cloak, a gift from the people of Covedrift on her sixteenth birthday, spun from the fleece of their hardy flock of white burrls. Potras glanced at her as she fastened it with a seashell brooch. "You'll need that, and maybe more, before this night is through," he said. He pointed. "Yonder is the first mark."

Amarynth squinted in the dim light. Ahead was an outthrust shoulder of stone, split cleanly down the middle by some shrug of the mountain. Just visible at the lip of the split was a single pale stroke of lighter material.

They rounded the mark and Amarynth looked into the shattered rock, where broken stone formed a natural, irregular staircase that climbed steeply fifty feet or more up the Crag before ending where the slope flattened slightly.

"You should see the second mark once you reach the top of this first stretch," Potras said.

"How high does this trail go?" Amarynth asked, studying the slope.

"To the top of the Crag. But it's far from straight.

You must follow the marks carefully. They glow in the dark, very slightly; Talus wanted to be able to use the path even at night—but he knew where to look, and what lay between. Make certain you have found the next mark before you leave one and be very cautious about where you put your feet and hands."

"I will." Amarynth heard a commotion downhill and glanced back at the cottage. Torches flickered in the forest below it. "They're coming," she said. "I'd better go —and so had you."

Potras reached out and clasped her hand. "Thank you. For my daughter..."

Amarynth heard Timara's frightened cry in the back of her mind, and turned sharply away, pulling free. "The Wanderer will have you if you don't get into the forest."

"Goodbye!" Elessa called softly after her; then they were gone, and Amarynth settled her pack more firmly and began to climb.

The ascent up the "staircase" of broken rock was relatively easy, and in just a few minutes she reached the second mark. There she paused, the wind tugging at her cloak, and stared up into the twilight, for the first time fully grasping the enormity of what she had begun.

Beyond the mark the slope gentled, creating a sixty-foot-wide shelf. Amarynth could see the third mark off to her right. But she could also see clearly the mass of granite towering over her, and for a moment her heart quailed.

The Crag loomed black against the dark grey clouds,

disquietingly like the Beast of the Between World rushing to engulf her. Thunder rumbled against it, closer than before, and the wind keened through cracks in the rock and the twisted branches of the stubborn, stunted trees that clung to it. *How can I climb this in the dark?* she thought despairingly. *This is no sea-cliff!*

She half-turned, thinking to descend and take her chances in the forest, when suddenly someone thrust a torch into the cleft below her, and she saw the pale face of a man, looking up at her unseeing. Behind him a Black Guard looked to his right as though awaiting his fellows.

Doubts abandoned, Amarynth scuttled across the shelf, which was not as flat as it had first appeared, to the third mark, and looked around quickly for the next. It glowed directly overhead, how far away she could not tell, for full night was upon her and that distant light could as easily have been on the moon as on the Crag.

She started up the granite wall, feeling for handholds. Her breathing rasped in her throat. The wall was rough and broken at its base, but as she ascended foot by foot, the stone smoothed, and soon each hold seemed to take forever to find, as she felt the rock to the limit of her outstretched fingertips in a slow arc. But always there *was* a hold, sometimes natural, sometimes chipped out of the granite by Talus's chisel, and so she climbed steadily, though expecting at any instant to hear the sound of pursuit.

Why are they delaying? she thought at one point.

They must not be sure I came this way, she answered herself some time later.

Such thoughts came in distinct, far-apart pulses; in between there was only the climb, the feel for each hold, and that glowing stroke above her, which never seemed any closer.

Her right arm developed an alarming tremor, pain gripped her left calf, and her fingertips were bruised and bleeding, so that every time she pulled herself up it felt like someone was driving splinters under her nails. The wind grew ever stronger, though at least it came from her back, pushing her against the rock; and the nearing sound of thunder was now accompanied by faint flickers of lighting, too dim to show her where next to put foot or hand.

Then, suddenly, she reached out with her left hand and found only empty space. It was so unexpected she jerked back, and her left foot broke free. As her body swung back into emptiness, she scrabbled frantically and latched onto something that was not stone, but wood—a root! Praying it would hold, she let it bear her weight, and pulled herself up onto a narrow ledge.

The mark she had been following for so long glowed only five or six feet above her, on an outthrust bit of the Crag.

For a moment, she lay on her back on the cold stone, beneath the lonely bush whose root had saved her, flexing sore fingers and toes, muscles twitching. *Grandfather,* she thought, *there were some things missing from my education.*

And then she heard a noise from below, and the breath stopped in her throat. She thrust her head over the lip of the ledge and listened.

There could be no mistaking the sound of someone climbing after her—someone climbing much faster than she had—*someone who must have the eyes of a nightswift*, she thought, for she could hear little hesitation in that ascent.

She scrambled to her feet. The next mark was to her right, and not much higher—and a helpful flash of lightning, the brightest yet, showed her that the ledge extended to it, wide as a pathway where she stood, narrowing to little more than a boot's breadth at its end, where there was a dark rift that Amarynth thought, in that single glimpse she had, widened higher up, perhaps extending all the way to the top of the Crag.

Whoever was climbing after her was getting close— much too close. Amarynth hurried along the ledge as fast as she dared, emptiness drawing in on her with every step. While still several feet from the mark, she was forced to put her back to the wall and slide sideways, the stone shrinking away beneath her.

And then, she discovered she had misjudged. The ledge did not extend all the way to that promising split in the rock. It ended three feet short, forcing her to stop, back pressed against the cliff. The glowing mark, so near but out of reach, seemed to taunt her.

Amarynth saw clearly what she had to do: turn around on the narrow ledge, lean into the Crag, and take a step over emptiness, trusting that her foot would find purchase inside that black opening.

She tried to swallow, but her mouth was too dry. For a long moment she just stood there, her thoughts not of the Black Guards pursuing her, the Wanderer, or even the Beast, but of her own room in Covedrift Tower, of the view from her window, of moonlight and sunlight and rain on the sea.

A sky-rending flash of lightning, followed in an instant by a shattering crack of thunder, snapped her back to the unpleasant here-and-now. She crept back along the ledge until there was room to turn around to face the cliff. Then, cheek pressed against the Crag, she edged back to the cleft. She took one last look behind her, just as lightning again streaked the sky—and in its garish light, she saw a dark shape pull itself onto the ledge and turn toward her.

An instant later, another burst of light revealed the baleful glitter of eyes in a pale face.

Gasping, she turned her head back toward the cleft and blindly swung out her foot. It banged against rock, and for a moment she teetered; then it thrust solidly into place. She stretched out her right hand and her fingers gripped the rock at the crack's edge. She started to pull herself into the narrow opening—

—and a gloved hand clamped around her left wrist.

Amarynth screamed and whipped her head around, coming face to face in a thunderclap with a man with eyes as black as the abyss below and teeth bared in a feral snarl. His back was pressed to the stone and his booted feet hung half-off the ledge, but, hanging onto her with the determination of a korg choking its prey, he began to pull her back, threatening to yank her arm from its socket if she did not release her hold in the cleft.

Fear and anger boiled up in Amarynth. With strength born of terror, she jerked her arm free. Pulled off balance, the man teetered, face still blank with hate; then he vanished, plummeting silently into the darkness, thunder masking the sound of his fall.

Amarynth gasped for air, suddenly weak; then, feeling her own hold slipping, made a supreme effort and pulled her whole body into the rift.

Above her, she saw the next mark, and in lightning-glare saw the path she had to walk to reach it. Her mind whirled like the storm clouds, because *she had seen it before*, in the Between World: it was the place where she had failed, where she had seen her grandfather's ghost and turned back from the Path, where the Beast had come upon her!

"That wasn't real," she whispered. "It wasn't!" But still, it took all her courage to get to her feet and begin to climb toward it.

The wind moaned and howled, and before she had gone ten feet the skies opened. Rain mixed with sleet drenched her, soaking through her cloak in an instant. Near-blind, shivering, she crawled up the slope on all fours, knowing she must be nearing the place where her grandfather had appeared in the Between World.

Not wanting to look but unable not to, she raised her head. As the rain poured into her eyes, lightning exploded overhead—and in the very place where she had seen her grandfather's dying form in the Between World, she saw a figure silhouetted against the suddenly bright sky, black cloak flapping in the gale.

Amarynth screamed.

The figure leaped down the slope toward her. Terror seized her throat, choking her into silence. She couldn't breathe, couldn't think. She reared back. Her foot slipped. She fell.

Something struck an enormous blow to the back of her head, and then, as though the Beast in the Between World had caught her after all, darkness swallowed her.

CHAPTER 8

The Beast was hunting. Amarynth knew it, could feel it in her bones. She cowered in a barren cave on a windswept shore, the sky storm-wracked above the tossing grey sea. In her arms she held Timara, who cried hopelessly and endlessly. Outside, she knew the shapeless monster was searching for her, and when suddenly a shape blocked the cave door, plunging her into darkness, she screamed—

—and awoke, jerking upright and cracking her forehead against something so hard she fell back again, her head and assorted other parts of her body throbbing with pain.

"Ow!" someone said, and she opened her eyes to see a boy about her own age gingerly touching his bleeding lip. Behind him, through an open window, she saw blue skies and a snow-capped peak. "Some thanks," the boy muttered. "I risk my life to save her and she loosens my teeth."

"I'm sorry," Amarynth whispered hoarsely.

The boy lowered his hand. "You *are* awake!"

"Now," she croaked. She gingerly felt the front of her head, which she'd just smashed onto the boy's mouth, and then the back of her head, where an aching lump greeted her questing fingers. She pulled them away. "Could I—is there something I could drink?"

"Of course." He reached down beside the bed on which she lay, and a moment later held a ladle filled with cold water to her lips. She sipped eagerly, then, feeling slightly more awake but no less sore, lay back again, looking at her benefactor.

Tall and rangy, he wore battered leather, much-patched. A long dagger with an unadorned black hilt hung in a plain brown sheath from his belt. Startling, light-green eyes gazed at her from a thin, tanned face, surrounded by shaggy black hair that looked as if he simply hacked it away with a knife whenever it got too long. "So," he said. "My name is Kalar. Who are you, why were you using Talus's path—and why did you scream when you saw me?"

For a moment Amarynth didn't reply, taking stock of her situation. She wore only her light undergarment, her Emblem tucked out of sight against her skin, where she had put it when she started climbing the Crag. Her clothes were spread to dry by the big stone hearth, in which burned a cheery fire. *He must have taken them off me,* she thought. *How embarrassing.* Out loud, all she said was, "How long have I been asleep?"

"It's only the next morning. Answer my questions."

She considered some more. If she told Kalar who she was, he might turn her over to the Black Guard. On the other hand, he *had* saved her life, and the Black Guards must still be searching for her. He deserved to know what trouble he might face for harbouring her. She compromised. "My name is Amarynth. And I was climbing the Cragway to escape the Black Guards. I screamed because you terrified me. I guess I slipped and hit my head as I fell." She touched her throbbing temple. She said nothing, for the moment, about the vision of her grandfather.

Kalar's eyes narrowed. "Black Guards are after you? Why?"

"How do I know you aren't their ally?" Amarynth countered.

The boy's fists clenched. "If I were a friend of the Black Guard, I would not be living in this hovel!" he snarled. "I am the son of Estar, Guesthost of Snowdeep!"

Amarynth's eyes widened. Next to the Spirit Singer and the elders, the Guesthost was the most powerful person in any village, for it was he (or she) who had the sacred responsibility of keeping an inn for travellers. The Guesthost could requisition goods from anyone; a guest's comfort came before the host's, and the Guesthost represented everyone in the community. Also, the Guesthost was always the first to hear the news of the outside world and heard it more completely, and was therefore often called upon by the elders when decisions had to be made.

"Then why *are* you here?" she asked. "And what does that have to do with the Black Guards?"

Kalar glared at her. "Why should I tell you?"

"Because I dare not tell you who I am until I know who you are," she replied simply.

Kalar's jaw clenched—but then he visibly forced himself to relax. He took a deep breath. "Very well." He pulled a simple wooden chair from beside an equally plain table, the room's only furnishings aside from the bed, and sat down beside her.

"Snowdeep is a village in a pass a week's journey from here," he began. "It's larger than Cragshadow because the pass offers the shortest route between several villages on opposite sides of the mountains. Due to the number of travellers, the Guesthouse is large, and the Guesthost a very important citizen. In some villages, such a Guesthost might abuse his position, taking things for his own pleasure instead of for his guests. But my father was not like that!" He glared at Amarynth as though daring her to contradict him. She said nothing.

"Our Spirit Singer, Aktal, was very old, near eighty, respected but not well-loved." Kalar made a face. "Respected by *others*. For my part, I had little use for him or the nonsense he proclaimed." He rapped the edge of his chair with his fist. "What I can see and hear and touch, that's what I believe in. If a few more people had felt the same way we could have done without a Spirit

Singer altogether and been far better for it—because the old Death Squawker brought it all upon us!

"Aktal had no apprentice and no family and claimed no child with the so-called Gift had been born in any nearby village in all his days. 'I grow old,' he told us in a village conclave one night, 'and Snowdeep must have a Spirit Singer to replace me when my days are done.' Because of that, he said, he had decided to send to Havenheart, to the Temple of the One, where he had heard several Singers were training."

Amarynth frowned. She knew of the temple in the far-away city of Havenheart, but not as a place of training Singers. It had always been the responsibility of Singers to find their own replacement, as her grandfather had found her. The temple had been built less than a hundred years ago as a centre of worship for the city's population, and her grandfather had expressed nothing but scorn for it. "Worship is a matter of the heart," he told her once. "You can—and should—worship every day, and anywhere. It doesn't require tall pillars, and gold chains, and priests growing fat off the offerings of their misguided followers."

Kalar continued, oblivious to her thoughts. "Aktal died suddenly one night. No one saw it happen. His death was announced the next morning by a man in a black robe, with a Spirit Singer's Emblem around his neck, who emerged from Aktal's dwelling, a dumpy little tower overlooking the pass, accompanied by four armed, armoured, and silent guards, also dressed in black. This stranger said Aktal's heart had failed. Even then, even before we knew what the Wanderer and the Black Guards were like, some of us were suspicious.

"The man said he was the Spirit Singer Aktal had sent for, a new kind of Spirit Singer, a 'Wanderer.' He gave no name, claiming to have renounced it to show his humility and obedience to the One, but said he had been sent by the greatest Spirit Singer of all, a man named Ar-Naathon, who, he said, 'is my spiritual guide, and that of all the people of the city of Havenheart.'" Kalar snorted. "Ar-Naathon. What kind of name is that?"

Amarynth's frown deepened. It *was* an odd name, but it sounded somehow familiar. Before she could chase down the elusive memory in her aching head, though, Kalar carried on.

"This 'Wanderer' set himself up in Aktal's old tower. Shortly after that he started going from house to house, always with his silent Black Guards, asking for more food, more hides and furs and wool and wine, more of everything, so that he could 'serve' better. At first the people gave, but when he returned, and it became obvious this was no one-time request but something new and permanent, he began to run into opposition.

"It was Jilha, the blacksmith, who finally drew the line. I was in his shop, getting a guest's therras re-shod, when the Wanderer came in with his Black Guards, as silent and faceless as basalt peaks. The Wanderer told Jilha he required 'bags of grain, iron ingots, arrowheads, and any weapons which you may have recently forged—

in order to serve you better,' and Jilha got very red in the face. 'You'll get nothing from me,' he roared. 'You're no true Spirit Singer—you're a bloodsucker! Get out of my smithy!' He reached out one hand, big as a boulder, and seized the Wanderer's black robe—and a Black Guard drew his sword and struck off his head.

"Then the Guard turned toward me, sword dripping with Jilha's blood, and I ran, leaving the therra, screaming, 'They've killed Jilha! They've killed Jilha!'" He snorted. "I thought the villagers would rise up, throw the Wanderer out. There were only four Black Guards, after all; they couldn't stand against a hundred of us. Bows would make short work of them, if it came to that.

"But as I ran, shouting, I saw people I had known all my life turn away and close and bolt their doors. I saw windows shuttered, shops closing—no one would help." His face hardened. "They were afraid—afraid of having a village without a Spirit Singer. They would let the Wanderer rob them of everything, even let the Black Guards murder a neighbour, because they didn't have the courage to die without someone moaning over them.

"All except my father." Kalar stopped. His lip trembled. It made him look younger and more vulnerable than he had so far. When he continued, his voice had roughened. "My father heard my shouts and came out into the courtyard of the Guesthouse. When he heard my breathless tale he took up a pitchfork and strode into the street, while I hid in an alleyway and watched.

"I saw the Wanderer and his Black Guards emerge

from Jilha's, leading the therra I had left behind. My father roared, 'Wanderer! That beast belongs to one of my guests!'

"The Wanderer came down the street to where my father stood, a Black Guard leading the therra. 'This therra will help me serve the village better,' he said. 'It is ancient custom for the Singer to take what he needs.'

"'It is ancient custom for the Singer to be *given* what he needs,' my father told him. I could hear the anger in his voice. 'It is *your* custom to take. You have taken Jilha's life. That is a matter for the elders. But now you have taken a therra that belongs to my guest, and that is a matter for *me*. Guest-custom is far more ancient than this new custom of yours, Wanderer. Give me the therra.'

"'And if I do not?' said the Wanderer.

"'Then I will do what I must and defend my guest's property,' said my father. He raised his voice to a shout. 'People of Snowdeep! This man has taken a life and now breaks guestright! Will you not come to my aid?'

"I saw faces peering from windows, but no one came out. In that moment, it seemed to me that my father sagged, as though struck a heavy blow. Still, he did not falter.

"'Then I will take it myself,' he said, and strode forward.

"I ran into the street, screaming at him to stay back, but he didn't even look at me. He reached out a hand to take the therra's bridle..." Kalar's voice trailed off.

"They killed him?" Amarynth whispered.

Kalar nodded, eyes down. "Two Black Guards ran him through, first one, then the other. He never even lifted the pitchfork. As he dropped to his knees, he half-turned toward me as though he were going to say something—and then he died. And the blood..." Kalar swallowed. "I ran. The Black Guard came toward me, and I ran. Out of Snowdeep, into the forest. They didn't follow me. They thought I wasn't worth it, I guess." For a moment Kalar just sat there, looking at the floor. Then he took a breath, straightened in his chair, and met Amarynth's eyes squarely. "That was six months ago," he said, his voice now hard and cold. "I wandered for weeks through snow and cold, half-starved, stealing from villages, always hiding from the Black Guards. Finally I found this hut. Talus knocked on the door after he blazed his trail. He told me his name and told me he was Spirit Singer of Cragshadow—but I said not a word to him and closed the door in his face. I'll have nothing more to do with Spirit Singers!"

For a moment only the crackle of the fire broke the silence of the hut. Then Kalar leaned forward. "So. You know my tale. You know I am no friend of the Black Guard. Now tell me who and what you are, and why you are fleeing them!"

Amarynth bit her lip, then slowly reached inside her shift and pulled out her Emblem.

CHAPTER 9

Kalar leaped to his feet, chair crashing to the floor. "*Spirit Singer!*" he hissed. "I might have known." He strode to the door, snagged his cloak from a peg on the wall, and flung it around his shoulders. "Stay here and rot," he said coldly. "I am done with you."

But as he turned to go, Amarynth said, "I am your guest."

Kalar froze, his hand on the doorpost. She saw his knuckles whiten. Then he spun, eyes glittering. "Witch! You know what that means to me."

"I do," Amarynth said. "If you are a true Guesthost, it means you can't leave me. It means you must take care of me. And it means you must listen to *my* story."

Lips pressed tight, Kalar very carefully undid the clasp holding his cloak in place. Folding the garment neatly, he laid it on the table. Amarynth read the suppressed tension in every movement, but wasn't about to relent; she needed help, and Kalar was all that was available.

He sat down again and faced her, his face drawn. "I'm listening," he growled.

Amarynth took a deep breath, then told him all that had happened, from the time her grandfather's nightmares began until she looked up and saw Kalar standing by the Path. "I must have glimpsed the future from the Between World," she said slowly. "Grandfather told me such things could happen, close to the Gate. I thought...I thought...you were the Beast, or in its service..." Her voice trailed off. Her head pounded. For a moment, the world seemed darker, and in the distance, she heard the cry of a lost child.

Kalar's expression remained closed. "So," he said. "You are having difficulty with your black arts. That is no concern of mine as Guesthost, and I'll thank you to keep your ravings on the matter to yourself. It is not my duty to listen to *them*. However, it seems you have managed to attract the attention of the Black Guards, and that *is* my concern.

"Therefore, while you are here, I will guard you with my life. But once you are well enough to leave, I will be finished with you and you with me. Understood?"

Amarynth's spirit fell at the chill in his tone. She had been hoping, naively, to gain an ally and companion for her quest—a quest that had gained even more importance. Now, more than ever, she *had* to find a true Singer, not only for her village but for all these blighted villages.

Somewhere, there had to be someone who knew how to fight these Wanderers and their master, the mysterious Ar-Naathon. But even if Kalar would not help her, it did not alter her duty. "Yes," she said wearily, and closed her eyes, and slept once more.

Late in the afternoon, she woke for the second time. She ate a simple supper given her by the silent, scowling Kalar, then slept again, coming half-awake only once in the full darkness of night, when Kalar came in from patrolling the Crag. He wrapped himself in blankets and stretched out on the floor beside her, and she dropped into sleep again.

She woke fully and suddenly some hours later when the door crashed open. Kalar shouted hoarsely. Struggling to free himself from the blankets, he scrambled awkwardly to his feet. She sat up, pain stabbing her head, to see a massive shape blocking the doorway. For a moment, hurting and sleep-befuddled, she thought it was the Beast itself, and she screamed, a scream that intensified an instant later as Kalar leaped at the form and was struck down by an all-too-solid sword hilt.

Then the figure leaned over her and a gauntleted hand seized her arm, fine mail links digging painfully into her flesh. She quit screaming, breath gone, as the Black Guard hauled her to her feet and half-led, half-dragged her out of the hut, over Kalar's crumpled body.

Barefoot, naked under her thin shift, Amarynth stumbled, shivering, through the cold mountain air. A million stars, brighter than she had ever seen them, burned uncaring in the sky. Amarynth wished with all her heart she were among them, anywhere but in this nightmare-come-to-life.

Her head throbbed and swum. She began to feel dizzy, tripping and falling, only to be hauled back to her feet by the Guard.

Finally, she blacked out completely. When she came to, the Guard had slung her over one armoured shoulder and was carrying her, buckles and bits of metal gouging her skin.

She drifted in and out of a sickly half-sleep, her head pounding in time with the Guard's steps; then became aware of growing light, and that they were travelling downhill, and finally heard the blowing and snuffling of therras and smelled wood smoke.

Abruptly the Guard stopped and dumped her unceremoniously on the ground. Her vision greyed; when she could see again, she found herself looking at a pair of booted feet beneath a long black robe, and slowly raised her head to look blearily at the man who stood over her.

The robe he wore was like that of a Spirit Singer, except for the colour. Around his neck he wore an Emblem, but it did not glow. Instead, it was black—not dark like Amarynth's, but *actively* black—an eye-hurting pit of darkness that seemed to suck the very light from the air.

"So, you're awake," the Wanderer said, echoing Kalar's first words to her. She wondered miserably if the boy still lived. "Excellent." The Wanderer's voice made

Amarynth think of a venomous sharss slithering over rock. She managed to sit up, and then to stand, swaying, leaning for support against the black wagon next to which she had been dropped. Behind her stood the Black Guard who had brought her there: another sat patiently at the reins of the wagon, and two others stood by three therras, one of which, she saw without surprise, was the beast she had brought from Covedrift. It rumbled at her unhappily. They were on a road which Amarynth guessed ran to Cragshadow; glancing behind her, she saw the Crag itself, more distant than she expected, thrusting up between two nearer hills.

She looked back at the Wanderer. Surprisingly young, he had a sallow, puffy face and a barely visible moustache. He licked his lips frequently and his eyes protruded slightly, like those of a swamp kribik, but despite his almost ludicrous appearance, she knew from Kalar what he was capable of.

"What do you want with me?" she said hoarsely.

"What do *I* want with you?" The Wanderer let his eyes rove down her thinly clad body, lingering on her bare legs and feet. She flushed but kept her gaze steady. "What I want with you is unimportant, unfortunately," he said, looking up again. "What is important is what Ar-Naathon wants."

"And what is that?" she demanded. "How does he even know about me? Havenheart is a long way from my village."

"Don't flatter yourself," the Wanderer said. "It is not

you he wants so much as it is any Spirit Singer who is not yet his servant."

"No Spirit Singer would—"

"You'd be surprised," the Wanderer said. "Some have been reluctant to pledge fealty, it's true. Their village find themselves in sudden need of a new Spirit Singer. Fortunately, we Wanderers stand ready to serve."

"You kill them?" Amarynth had thought she couldn't be any more horrified than she already was. She'd been wrong.

The Wanderer shrugged, as if such slaughter did not matter in the least. "You and others like you—apprentices—are special. Lucky you." He smiled, not at all pleasantly. "Ar-Naathon can mould you more easily."

"We'll see about that!" Amarynth said, but her bravado sounded thin and childish in her own years.

"Oh, we certainly will," agreed the Wanderer. "Now, get in the wagon. You're going to the city."

Amarynth didn't move. "I'd like a cloak. I'm cold."

"I think not," the Wanderer said. He leered at her. "I like you as you are."

"And what will your Master say if I'm sick when you bring me to him?"

The Wanderer's eyes narrowed, and she knew she'd scored a hit, however minor. He harrumphed, then turned to the wagon. He rummaged in a trunk in the back for a moment, then turned to fling a long black cloak of exquisite make to her. She wrapped it around her, shutting out the cold morning air at last. "Black's hardly my favourite colour," she said.

"It will be," the Wanderer snapped. "Now get in the wagon!"

This time Amarynth obeyed, climbing into the back while the Wanderer sat beside the Black Guard who held the reins. The remaining Black Guards mounted their therras. As the wagon lurched forward, they spread out around it, one riding ahead, one ranging from side to side, and one riding directly behind her.

Sitting among bags and boxes and trunks looted from the mountain villages, huddled in her borrowed cloak, Amarynth found herself staring straight into the eyeholes of the trailing Black Guard's helmet, remembering the hate-filled face of the man who had pursued her up the Cragway and died so silently. Had he been a Black Guard without his armour, or some other unfortunate servant of the Wanderer?

She looked past the Black Guard, then, at the dwindling Crag. "I'm sorry, Kalar," she whispered. "I should have let you go when you wanted to."

Her head still throbbed, and her filthy body ached. She lay down, pillowed her head on a grain sack, wrapped the black cloak more tightly around her, and slowly sank into a fitful, unrestful slumber, while the wagon rumbled on toward the distant city—and the Wanderer's mysterious master.

❧

CHAPTER 10

Through the two-week journey that followed, Amarynth learned just how far Ar-Naathon's power had spread. In every village they were met by Black Guards and Wanderers—and closed shutters and barred doors. At first her own Wanderer continued to make lewd taunts at every opportunity, but Amarynth made it clear she knew he dared not touch her, and after a day or two he relented and instead ignored her, except to occasionally give her orders.

During the day she lay in the wagon or sat facing backward with her feet dangling, watching the mountains give way to rolling hills and finally to fertile, cultivated plains. Villages became more and more numerous as they travelled south, and traffic more common on the road— tradesmen and traders, farmers going to market, and herdsmen with flocks of woolly burrls or lumbering herds of great red knaxen. All shrank from the black wagon and its escort, except for the occasional Black Guards, who paid them no mind at all. Amarynth watched everything with interest sharpened by a forlorn hope of escape, but the Black Guards were always nearby, and she knew from Kalar just how unlikely it was that anyone who saw her fleeing the Black Guards would try to aid her.

Sometimes during the long nights, locked in a room alone or forced to share one with the Wanderer, wondering if his lust would overpower his fear of his Master, she imagined Kalar coming after her, somehow eluding the Black Guards and rescuing her, taking her back to safety in some hidden corner of the mountains. Sometimes she imagined it so strongly she almost convinced herself it would happen.

But always the light of day brought cold reason to bear, and she knew her hopes were foolish. If Kalar still lived—and the worst of it was, she didn't know and might never know—he would have no reason to come after her, and every reason not to. She had forced herself on him by appealing to his father's memory, had brought the Black Guards to his hiding place, and in the end had got him knocked in the head. Plus, she was a Spirit Singer—a "Death Squawker," in his crude words—and therefore connected in his mind with the one whom he blamed for what had happened in his village. No doubt her disappearance was good riddance, as far as he was concerned.

It wasn't only her foolish imagination and her fear of

the Wanderer that kept her from sleeping at nights. When she did doze, her dreams were uniformly bad, filled with dreadful images of the Beast, of her grandfather, of Davin—and always, always, Timara's bitter crying, flooding her with doubt and self-reproach. It did no good to tell herself she was only an apprentice Singer. She felt if only she hadn't turned back on the Path, the Beast would not have come, and she would have reached the Gate with the child.

She tried to make up for unrestful nights by dozing miserably in the back of the wagon, wakened by every bump or turn, either baking in the sun that grew increasingly hot, or soaked and shivering on those days when rain and mist swept over the plain. She begged the Wanderer for more clothes, but he only scowled at her. "I've already wasted as fine a cloak as you'll ever wear," he snapped. "You'll have nothing else."

By the end of the two weeks it sometimes seemed to Amarynth that all her former life had been a dream, and that she had spent all her days swaying in the back of a black wagon, bound for some mysterious destination that never seemed to get any closer.

But late one afternoon they swung toward the setting sun and came to a stone bridge spanning a broad, slow-moving river. They rattled up the rounded cobblestones and stopped at the top of the arch, where the Wanderer pointed upstream. "The City of Havenheart," he said with a wicked grin. "We'll have you in Ar-Naathon's hands tonight—though I'd rather you were in mine."

Amarynth hardly heard the jibe; she was staring along the glimmering length of the placid river to the towers that rose like a mirage miles away. In the sun's last light they seemed made of gold, glowing against a backdrop of distant black peaks, windows shining like sparks of fire. A trio of white birds flew overhead, calling single notes in high, clear voices, leading the way to the city.

Names came to Amarynth from her grandfather's long-ago geography lessons. The river was the Lifeblood, and those far-away mountains to the south were the mysterious Haunted Range, where ghosts of the unSung were said to walk and few men dared go.

The wagon lurched forward, the sun set, and the city vanished into twilight.

They reached the city gate in darkness an hour later. Amarynth stared at it, astonished. She had seen drawings of Havenheart in her grandfather's library, and it had always seemed to her like a village grown beyond all reason. Sprawling astride the Lifeblood, it was the place where the First Landers had settled, after marching across the barren western hills from the sea. Though most had scattered across the continent, many had stayed in that first town of the new land. It had become a centre of trade, and later, when the temple was built, a centre of worship, and had always been open to anyone who would enter, as open as any village with a thousandth of its population.

No longer. A frowning wall, twelve feet tall, loomed over them. Set amongst the massive stones was a gate of iron, guarded by towers to either side and armed men before—but not, Amarynth saw, Black Guards. The surcoats of these men were blue, as were the plumes that topped the spikes of their round steel helmets. Their silvered armour gleamed red in the light of the torches set in iron brackets beside the gate. As the wagon trundled forward, archers appeared in the windows of the towers, arrows nocked, and one of the soldiers before the gate drew his sword and came forward. "Halt!" he commanded, and the Black Guard tugged on the reins.

As the soldier looked up at the Wanderer, his eyes widened slightly. But his voice was brusque as he said, "Your name?"

"I am the Wanderer Elsdar, newly returned from the Mountains of the North," said Amarynth's captor, his voice haughty. It was the first time she had heard his name, or even known he had one. "Let me pass."

"In a moment." The soldier nodded at Amarynth. "Who is she?"

"A prisoner of Ar-Naathon," snapped Elsdar. "Perhaps you would like to question the master, too?"

The soldier stepped back. "Open the gate!" he shouted toward the tower, then stood aside, scowling, as the massive door swung open and the Black Guard drove the wagon through.

The gate let them into a narrow passage between the towers, pierced with numerous slit windows. A second gate at the far end of the passageway also swung open, and they clattered into a cobblestoned courtyard surrounded by low white buildings. Across from them, a torchlit street meandered away among houses, shops, and guesthouses, their windows aglow with lantern-light.

A door in a building to their left suddenly swung open. Out strode a young man, armoured like the soldiers but dressed in white instead of blue. He carried his helmet carelessly by its spike with his right hand, and his short blonde hair gleamed in the torchlight like gold.

The Wanderer, seeing him, stopped the wagon, clambered down, and knelt on the cobblestones. "Prince Ka-Raamon," he murmured.

"Oh, stand up, stand up, Elsdar," said the prince, waving a nonchalant hand. "You know I hate that sort of thing."

"Yes, Your Highness." Elsdar scrambled to his feet but kept his head bowed. Ka-Raamon brushed past him and circled to the back of the wagon, his eyes locked on Amarynth.

She stared at him, astonished. Whoever she had expected to greet her in Havenheart, it wasn't a brash boy with a charming grin and startling blue eyes. And that hair! She had never seen hair that colour.

"Spirit Singer Amarynth, I presume," he said, his teeth flashing in a grin. "Let me help you down."

She ignored his proffered hand, instead clambering down by herself. Feet bare on the cold cobblestones, she wrapped her cloak more tightly around her. The boy bowed to her. "Prince Ka-Raamon, your servant."

She looked at him with mistrust. "How do you know my name?"

"We received word of your coming several days ago. There are faster means of travel than a wagon, you know." He settled his helmet on his head, and Amarynth saw that its plume was as golden as his hair. Then he crooked his arm. "Allow me to escort you to my father's palace."

She didn't move. "Your father?"

"Ar-Naathon, of course." He smiled. "Come."

Elsdar stepped forward. "Your Highness, my orders are to escort all captured Spirit Singers personally to—"

Ka-Raamon turned toward him, still smiling. "Elsdar, are you questioning my authority?"

The Wanderer paled and fell back a step. "N-no, Your Highness."

"Most glad to hear it. Run along, then. Thank you for bringing Amarynth."

"Yes, Your Highness. Thank you, Your Highness." After bowing deeply, Elsdar hurriedly remounted the wagon. Then he growled an order to the driver, who, like the other Black Guards, had remained impassive throughout the exchange. The wagon and its escorting riders clip-clopped off into the city

Ka-Raamon turned toward Amarynth. "I trust your journey was pleasant?"

Amarynth gave him her coldest stare. "Prince Ka-Raamon, it is hardly pleasant to be taken prisoner, bundled into a wagon, and brought against my will on a two-week journey to a place I never wished to visit."

"Never wished to visit?" The prince seemed astonished. "But, Amarynth, this city is the most marvellous place in Haven! Especially since my father became master." He reached out and took her hand. "I must take you to him, but there are many things I can show you on the way…"

Amarynth shook her head but followed, limping as she crossed the hard stones. The prince noticed at once and stopped, looking down at her bare feet in surprise. "Why, where are your shoes?"

"I was in bed when I was taken prisoner," she said shortly. "Elsdar gave me this cloak; otherwise I have nothing to wear but a light shift. He didn't even let me grab my pack before we left."

"Unforgivable," the prince said. "I'll have him punished for it—I'll make him walk ten times around the palace, barefoot to his chin, while you watch. In the winter!"

Amarynth laughed despite herself. "Please don't," she said. "He never actually hurt me, and I rode in the wagon the whole way."

"Well." The prince hardly looked mollified. "Perhaps I can help. In addition to my rooms in the palace, I have quarters down here—right over there, in fact." He pointed to the door through which he had emerged. "I have a young squire about your size—you can wear some of his clothes, and a pair of his boots, just until we get to the palace. Then I'll have you properly dressed by the finest seamstresses in the city."

Amarynth hesitated but could see no choice but acceptance. "Thank you, Prince Ka-Raamon."

"Please, call me Ramon," said the prince. "Ka-Raamon is—well, I love my father, but he does have very strange taste in names." He led her toward his quarters. "Though Ka-Raamon is better than Ar-Naathon, at that. And I have a baby sister he named Isla-Theodis, if you can believe it."

"Didn't your mother object?" Amarynth asked, but the prince didn't seem to hear her.

"Here we are!" he said cheerfully, swinging open the door. The room beyond was warmly lit by brass lanterns hanging from dark wooden beams, and richly decorated, with carved chairs upholstered in blue velvet, white, deep-piled carpet, an incredibly broad bed, and a wardrobe made of polished wood that glowed like gold. From that wardrobe the prince drew out a finely woven seamless undertunic, a white overtunic trimmed in gold, a blue cloak, gold trousers, and a pair of soft grey boots.

"I suppose a bath is out of the question," Amarynth said wistfully, looking at the clean clothing and contrasting it with her soiled self.

The prince grinned. "Not at all!" He went to a door in the back of the room and opened it with a flourish, revealing a second, smaller chamber, mostly taken up by a sunken marble tub. He turned a golden spigot in the wall and steaming water spurted.

Amarynth gasped. "How do you do it?"

"A fire in a central room, water from a well. We like to give our men-at-arms a few privileges—it makes them fight better."

Amarynth was looking forward to a bath and clean clothes so much that the question *Fight whom?* only flickered across her mind.

When the tub was filled, the prince showed her towels stacked nearby, bowed, and said, "I'll be waiting in the courtyard." He went out, closing the bathroom door behind him; a moment later, she heard the front door close, as well.

At once, Amarynth dropped her cloak and pulled her torn, filthy shift over her head. As she stepped into the tub the water felt delightful, but just for a moment she froze, half in and half out, feeling certain she was being watched. She shot a glance at the bathroom door, but it was firmly closed and there were no windows.

Comes from being around Elsdar too long, she thought, and let the blessed caress of the clean, hot water flow around her weary body.

CHAPTER 11

Bathed and dressed in the clothes the prince had provided—a tad long in the arms and tight in the chest, but far better than what she had been wearing—Amarynth emerged into the courtyard to find Ka-Raamon on the porch with his back to a pillar and his feet drawn up, idly playing the children's game of Stars and Moons on the planking with a bit of charcoal. When the door opened he looked up, then grinned. "A vision of loveliness!" he proclaimed. "Which is more than I can say for the squire who usually wears those clothes," he added as he got to his feet.

Amarynth laughed. "Thank you, Prince Ka-Raamon."

"Ramon, Ramon, remember?" The prince held out his arm, and this time Amarynth took it, telling herself that whether he proved to be friend or foe, there was no point in antagonizing him—and so far, at least, he had been kind.

He led her out of the courtyard and down the torchlit street. "You wouldn't believe it to look at it now," he said as they walked, "but I've been told Havenheart was little more than an overgrown village when my father became Master of the City. No walls, few stone buildings except for the temple, and a few dozen men-at-arms in worn-out armour lazily patrolling the streets—which were usually muddy." He gestured proudly around. "Now look at it! Only twenty years have passed, and it's finally starting to look as grand as its size!"

It *was* impressive, Amarynth had to admit. Many buildings were still of wood and plaster, but many others were of smooth white or red stone, and the cobbles of the courtyard continued beneath their feet, clattering as wagons and therras passed to and fro. Not only that, but the street was clean—"Washed every day by the people whose property fronts it," the prince explained proudly. He pointed to the broad gutter down the street's centre. "That empties into an underground aqueduct, which eventually leads down-river." He laughed. "The most trouble I ever got into as a child was the day when I went exploring in the sewer and turned up in the middle of one of my father's conferences dripping wet and smelling not at all like a prince!"

Amarynth smiled again, and smiled more and more as they continued down the street, beginning, despite her doubts and uncertain situation, to enjoy the unaccustomed pleasure of having someone near her age to talk and laugh with.

Of course, Kalar and Davin had also been close to her in age, but there was no comparison between the one's dour bitterness and hostility and the other's shy friendliness, and Ka-Raamon's—*Ramon's*, she corrected herself—openness and good humour. Ramon didn't seem to care that she was a Spirit Singer; he seemed to think of her only as a girl, and a rather pretty one at that, whom he was conducting to the palace to see his father.

It was hard to connect him with any of the bad things that had happened to her, and in any event, Amarynth was ready to forget bad things; and so she laughed at Ramon's jokes and tried not to think about what would happen when she at last met Ar-Naathon.

Havenheart continued to astonish her. Already they had travelled down one street farther than the distance between Covedrift and her grandfather's tower, and still they passed half-timbered houses, leaning over the cobblestones, guesthouses from which spilled laughter and music, shops closed for the night but bewildering in their profusion, selling everything from perfume to pork, and, squeezed in among the other buildings, strange little peak-roofed shelters in which red lamps glowed before two or three rows of benches.

Amarynth asked the prince about them.

"Shrines," he said, with some surprise. "Don't they have them up north?"

"Shrines?"

"For the worship of the One. On Temple Day we can't *all* fit in the temple, you know. And some people like to pop in for a prayer now and then any old day of the week."

Amarynth looked back at the one they had just passed. "Temple Day?"

The prince laughed. "You really have come a long way, haven't you? Yes, Temple Day. Once a month, everybody stops what they're doing to pray."

"Oh," said Amarynth, wondering why anyone needed a special day to pray—or a special place.

Ahead of them a building bulked over all others, its soaring towers and spires aglitter with lights like yellow stars. The prince pointed to it and grinned. "Home," he said. "The palace."

Staring up at those towers, Amarynth was suddenly jerked to one side by Ramon, who immediately apologized. "Sorry, sorry," he said, "but you almost walked into him."

"Who?" Amarynth glanced over her shoulder and saw a Black Guard striding down the street.

"They're a bit single-minded," explained Ramon. "He might not have bothered going around you."

The sight of that grim figure brought Amarynth rudely back to her situation—and the uncertainty of the prince's true nature. With Ar-Naathon's palace in sight, it was surely time to try to get some answers. "Just who or what *are* the Black Guards?" she asked. "They never talk, or laugh, or do anything normal men do—it's like there's a ghost inside that armour."

"Oh, forget them," said the prince. "Look—we're almost to the palace gate."

Which is precisely why I can't forget them, Amarynth thought, but said nothing more as they approached the gate, a smaller version of the one through which she had entered the city. This time there was no question of being stopped; the moment the prince stepped into the light of the multiple torches illuminating the gate, one of the blue-liveried men-at-arms turned and shouted inside, so the gate was open when they reached it. The prince strode through, telling the kneeling guards to "Stand up, stand up!", and they emerged into a courtyard green with well-cropped grass. A fountain leaped in a basin of white marble at its centre, waking musical echoes from the surrounding walls.

The creamy stones of those walls glowed pale gold in the light of torches, held aloft by silver sconces at frequent intervals. Ramon and Amarynth walked from pool to pool of light, circling the fountain to reach the palace itself, a great mass of white and red blocks. Towers rose where the courtyard wall and palace met, but the tallest tower of all soared much farther back, crowned with light by a ring of illuminated windows just beneath its peaked red roof. "Magnificent, isn't it?" said the prince to Amarynth as they approached the palace's cast-bronze doors. "My father only finished it this year."

They passed through the doors and between two

more blue-clad guardsmen into an enormous antechamber, from which two curved staircases swept up to the second floor. As they crossed the chamber, footsteps echoing, Amarynth glimpsed, off to their left, the high-ceilinged opulence of a great hall, but the prince led her to a much smaller door concealed behind one staircase, and through it into a plain stone corridor that arrowed into the palace's heart.

"My father doesn't really care for all that marble and gold," said Ramon as they strode along the hallway. "He only used it for show in the most public places." He smiled at Amarynth. "It's a shame, really, because I have rather a fondness for it."

The corridor ended in a simple wooden door, which Ramon opened with a key drawn from the leather pouch at his belt. Inside, a staircase spiralled upward, and Amarynth realized they had reached the central tower.

Though their entire way was well-lit by frequent lamps, Amarynth felt as if she were descending deeper and deeper into dark, dangerous places rather than ascending a tower of white stone. She remembered, only too well, all she had heard of Ar-Naathon from Potras and Kalar, of Spirit Singers "taken" or slain, of Wanderers who stole from the people, no doubt sending the loot back to Havenheart. The very tower she was climbing had likely been built with wealth stripped from the outlying villages.

She remembered her own captivity, and the Black Guard striking down Kalar to take her from the hut, and the blank-faced servant of the Wanderer who had plunged to his death while pursuing her up the mountain, and she pulled free of Ramon, who glanced at her in surprise. "Something wrong?"

Maybe he doesn't know what's being done in his father's name. She wanted to believe that. But though she said, "No," she didn't take his arm again.

The prince shrugged and started whistling a tune Amarynth thought sounded vaguely familiar. "What is that song?" she asked as they continued to climb.

Ramon broke off and blushed, which made him look very young. "Sorry," he said. "It's something I heard among the soldiers—I doubt you'd know it."

"You might be surprised," said Amarynth, amused and strangely touched by his discomfiture. *Surely he can't be as black as his father is portrayed.* "It sounds a lot like something I heard some fishermen singing once when they didn't know I was around."

Ramon laughed, but he didn't whistle any more.

A few seconds later they came to a landing and another door, and Ramon knocked sharply three times. Amarynth barely had time to take a deep breath to try to calm her pounding heart before the door opened, revealing a tall, thin man, dressed simply in dark-blue tunic and trousers. A servant, she thought—until Ramon turned to her, grinning, and said, "Spirit Singer Amarynth, may I present Ar-Naathon, Master of Havenheart...my father."

Amarynth gaped at Ar-Naathon, who smiled and

opened the door wider. "Come in, come in. I've been expecting you." His voice was surprisingly soft.

Bemused, Amarynth stepped into the circular room with Ramon. Ar-Naathon closed the door behind them. She looked around; despite Ar-Naathon's lofty title, the furnishings were of plain, dark wood, well-made but hardly luxurious. Windows with shutters flung wide surrounded them, letting the cool night breeze flow through unimpeded.

On the table was spread a vellum map of Haven, which Ar-Naathon quickly rolled up. "Won't you sit down?" he asked, gesturing to one of the chairs at the table, and as she did so, went on, "Can I get you anything? Wine? Water? Something to eat? I had my servant bring me a platter of bread and cheese and cold meats just a few minutes ago..."

"I—I am hungry, thank you," said Amarynth, and watched as the Master drew a pewter plate and mug from a cabinet, filled the mug with wine from a skin hung in the cooling breeze of the window, and returned to the table with it and the promised platter of food, which had been resting on a side table.

The prince sat on the bed. "I should have realized you'd be hungry," he said ruefully. "We could have eaten a dozen times on the walk up here."

Amarynth's mouth was too full to allow her to reply.

Ar-Naathon sat opposite her as she ate, watching, until finally she took a last swallow of the excellent wine —she'd drunk only half the glass; any more than that and her head would begin to spin—and pushed the plate away. "Thank you," she said. "I—I'm surprised."

"Surprised?" said Ar-Naathon. Despite his soft voice, his eyes had a disturbing, burning intensity.

"I wasn't exactly invited to supper," she pointed out. "I was brought here against my will by one of your Wanderers and four of your Black Guards, after being chased, captured, tied up, carried, and finally loaded in a wagon like a—a prize knax!" Her temper rose as she spoke. *An island of serenity*, she reminded herself, but her outrage was too great for her to be very serene. She folded her arms and waited to see what the Master of Havenheart would say.

"Oh, child, I'm so sorry." The soft voice purred like a mountain korg's kitten. "But rest assured, Elsdar will be punished."

"Elsdar? Elsdar is the smallest part of it! I came from Covedrift seeking your Wanderers in good faith, because I thought they must be Spirit Singers of great power, and instead—"

"But all your misfortunes were Elsdar's doing," Ar-Naathon said sadly. "All that district of the mountains fell under his sway. I had not realized how corrupt he had become. I have rebuked him before, and truly thought—well. I am too trusting." He sighed, as though at the vagaries of mankind. "The Black Guards are—simple men," he went on. "They obey without question. It's—their way. They were sent into the outer lands to help the Wanderers, who are not there to usurp the local Spirit

Singers, despite what you were told by those who knew only Elsdar, but only to teach them the new ways we have discovered here, to give them the power of Wanderers. Elsdar became greedy and tried to hide it by claiming all he did was by my decree." Ar-Naathon shook his head. "He used the Black Guards to terrorize and rob, to amass wealth for himself."

"For himself? Not for you?"

Ar-Naathon looked shocked. "Child! Of course not!"

"Why did the Black Guards seize me in the first place?"

"A Wanderer can sense when another Spirit Singer is nearby. Elsdar felt your presence and sent the Black Guards after you, no doubt fearing that with another Spirit Singer present, the people would no longer bow to his power over their souls but would rise up against him."

Amarynth shook her head stubbornly. "It doesn't make any sense. Why should Elsdar bring me to you, then? Why not just kill me?"

"He had no choice." Ar-Naathon spread his hands. "I am not only Master of the City, I am the First of Wanderers. Any Wanderer can sense the presence of a nearby Singer; I can sense the presence of Singers over a great distance. I sensed you. And all Wanderers have standing orders to bring new Singers to me—though it is supposed to be voluntarily. Fortunately for you, I didn't fully trust Elsdar, so I had Ka-Raamon meet you when you arrived. If I had not..." Ar-Naathon looked grim. "You would never have reached the palace. There are dangerous elements in this city, evil men and women who deny the worship of the One and the power of the Wanderers. Elsdar must have links to them. He could have arranged for an attack on himself in which you 'tragically' would have died, leaving him clear of suspicion—or, at least, of provable wrongdoing."

Amarynth swallowed. "Then—" She looked around at Ramon, who grinned at her. "Then Ramon—uh, Prince Ka-Raamon, saved my life?"

"In a manner of speaking," said the prince modestly. "But I assure you, it was well worth saving. I have most enjoyed accompanying you." He grinned suddenly. "And there's so much more to see in Havenheart. Tomorrow, I'll—"

"Not tomorrow," said Ar-Naathon firmly, and his son's face fell.

"Oh, of course," said the prince. "I wasn't thinking."

"Why not tomorrow?" asked Amarynth.

"Because tomorrow," Ar-Naathon said, "we must answer your questions in the only way possible. We must calm your fears concerning what you call the Beast, so you can go back to your village a true Singer."

Amarynth's heart beat faster. "You're going to end my apprenticeship?"

"Of course, little sister." His eyes glittered above his gentle smile. "Tomorrow, Amarynth, we are going to make you a Wanderer."

CHAPTER 12

In her chamber that night, overlooking the green courtyard and its softly splashing fountain, Amarynth could not sleep. She stood on her balcony, wrapped in a soft blue robe, only one of the beautiful garments that had been lying on the bed when the prince showed her to the room, and looked down at the guards making their rounds, the torchlight striking red sparks from their armour.

With her quest to be completed on the morrow and a soft bed awaiting her, she should have slept at once; but deep in her heart she was still troubled. The prince was gracious and kind and his father, far from being the ogre rumour had led her to expect, seemed courteous and knowledgeable. He had explained everything that had happened in the mountains, most reasonably.

But the whole concept of Wanderers was against

everything her grandfather had taught her about Spirit Singing, and worse, was an axe-blow to the very roots of Haven society. Whether Ar-Naathon wanted it or not (and she was not as certain of his lack of ambition as Ramon seemed to be), he was gathering immense power to himself—not just the power of a mighty Spirit Singer, though obviously that was his as well, but the power of a lord of men, the kind of lord that had not existed since men came to Haven. The First Landers had done away with lords and princes, with courts and retainers and all the hierarchy of power and influence that went with them. Every village ruled itself, selected its own leaders from among its own people, and was served by its own Spirit Singer.

Now, though, Havenheart had, not a council of elders, but a "Master of the City." (The very name sounded blasphemous to Amarynth's ears, for to a Spirit Singer, there was only one Master.) And this "master" had a son—a son called a prince, the ancient title for the son of a king. In everything but name, Ar-Naathon *had* made himself king, not just of the city but, through his Wanderers, of all Haven.

Yet if the Wanderers were truly what Ar-Naathon claimed, how could she fault him? Freeing people to travel and trade more easily could not be a bad thing. Look at the wealth it had already brought the city. It could generate new prosperity, throughout the land. Why should she fear that?

She smiled a little sadly. "We Spirit Singers are by nature conservative," she whispered her grandfather's words to herself. "Our truths are unchanging; we prefer to see the world remain unchanging, too. It's far more comfortable."

The smile faded. *We Spirit Singers*, she thought. *Tomorrow I'll be able to say that and mean it—if I can overcome my fear.* She looked up at the stars; though of course the Between World was everywhere around her, somehow she always thought of it as being above the sky. Somewhere out there in the cold shadows the Beast still waited. Tomorrow she would have to return to its realm, where Timara wailed, lost and alone.

That's what really frightens me.

Ar-Naathon had been vague about what to expect. "It will be much like your normal training," he had told her. "But with a slight variation. We have found a source of power in the Between World that has been lost for centuries. We will Link you to it—and then you will be a Wanderer."

"A Spirit Singer? Without ever making a solitary journey to the Gate?"

"With the power you will have, that won't be necessary," Ar-Naathon had replied.

She turned away from the window and returned to the bed, taking off the robe and laying it over a velvet-upholstered chair before slipping beneath the snow-white sheets of fine linen. She had tried to ask Ar-Naathon about the Beast, but the Master of the City had only smiled and told her all her questions would be answered on the morrow.

Their secret power must be great indeed if they don't fear the Beast, she thought, just before sleep claimed her.

In the morning she was awakened by a young maid with wide blue eyes in a pale, freckled face, who wouldn't speak to her despite her efforts to be friendly. Silent as a sea breeze, the girl brought in a tray of fruit and bread, then, while Amarynth ate, went into an adjoining room and filled a brass tub with hot water from a spigot like the one Amarynth had seen in Ramon's quarters by the city gate. When Amarynth emerged from the bath the maid met her with a towel and her blue robe, then showed her the clothes she was to wear for her ceremony, spread out on the newly made bed.

The main garment was a sleeveless, floor-length robe like the ceremonial one she had worn at home—which, she supposed, was still in her pack on the floor of Kalar's hut on the Crag—but dark blue, almost black, instead of white. There were also black undergarments and black sandals, and a belt made of silver links, fastened with a sapphire buckle.

Amarynth touched the Emblem around her neck, which she had not removed since leaving her grandfather's tower, even while bathing. *Will it live at last?* she wondered. Breath catching, she donned the clothing, while the maid stood by, eyes downcast.

The moment Amarynth was dressed, the maid opened the door, then scurried out as the prince entered, glittering in a red tunic, gold trousers, red boots, and a snow-white cape. A golden circlet, centred with a ruby on his forehead, bound his blonde hair. He smiled at her. "Good morning," he said. "A Wanderer's robe suits you."

She smiled back. "Thank you. The clothing of a prince suits you."

Ramon bowed, then offered her his arm. She took it and he led her into the corridor.

As they walked its sky-blue carpet, they passed more servants and men-at-arms, who hastened to fall back against the walls to let them pass, bowing deeply. The prince ignored them, but Amarynth found it disconcerting and not entirely pleasant to be bowed to, and remembered her thoughts of the previous night. With a glance at Ramon, she asked, "I've been wondering how you came by the title of prince, Ramon. It's as archaic as your name—there hasn't been a prince since the Landing. Doesn't it mean son of a king?"

Ramon laughed. "Indeed it does. But I didn't choose it; the people did. They were so grateful to my father for the wealth he brought the city, by creating Wanderers who could allow people to live and trade wherever they chose, that they would have made him king—except he wouldn't allow it. He was reluctant even to take the title of Master of the City, but they insisted, just as they insisted on building this palace for him; and even though he won't call himself king, that's how the people treat him. But nothing would stop them from calling me a prince—so prince I am."

Amarynth remembered hard eyes above Ar-Naathon's soft smile and thought Ramon had allowed his love of his father to blind him. The people might have thrust power upon Ar-Naathon, but she was more and more convinced he had not found it unwelcome. "But a prince becomes a king on the death of his father," she said lightly. "Does that mean you will be the first King of Havenheart?"

"I suppose it does," said Ramon without concern. "But my father is far from being an old man. I'm not going to worry about it for a long, long time." They reached the end of the corridor and the head of the sweeping stairs into the main entry chamber, crowded with people hurrying hither and yon, in sharp contrast to the previous night's emptiness. As Amarynth and the prince descended, people stared, hurried out of the way, then turned and bowed, just as in the corridor. Ramon and Amarynth crossed the gold-inlaid marble floor and went out into the courtyard, the blue-clad men-at-arms at the door snapping to attention as they passed, black-hafted spears thudding against the pavement.

"A lovely day, isn't it?" said the prince, taking a deep breath of the morning air. "A bit cool now, but it will warm up later." He waved negligently as they approached the palace gate and it swung open at once.

Amarynth, contrasting Ramon's comment the night before that he hated people bowing to him with his easy assumption of a royal manner this morning, glanced at him sharply, wondering for the first time if perhaps he, too, was less unconcerned about his exalted rank than he claimed. *It's as if he's playing roles. Last night, he was a simple young man made a prince through no wish of his own, making the girl from the fringes of Haven feel welcome in the city through his own unassuming nature. Today, he's a foppish lordling accepting all the honour without question.* She wondered if she had seen the real Ramon yet, or the real Ar-Naathon, and the notion reawakened the night's uncertainties.

The cobblestoned courtyard beyond the palace gate, deserted the night before, was now a riot of people and animals. A ponderous wagon loaded with wine barrels trundled by noisily in one direction, pursued by shouting children playing tag, while a dainty carriage carrying a veiled woman rolled by in the other. Merchants vied to outshout each other in proclaiming their wares. Sparks showered the stones at Amarynth's feet from the wheel of a nearby knife grinder and a fat old woman carrying a basket of bread gave her a gap-toothed grin as she limped by. It was all Amarynth could do not to stare open-mouthed—she had never seen so many people.

They all stood aside for the prince, bowing deeply as he passed, so that a path opened as if by magic before them as they crossed the courtyard and entered a street that paralleled the palace wall. "It's not far to the temple," the prince told Amarynth as the tag-playing children scuttled out of their way. "My father won't be there, but one of his most trusted Wanderers will greet us and prepare you for the ceremony—and answer any questions you may have."

Amarynth nodded, feeling again a little shiver of—fear? nervousness?—but as she did so, something caught her attention out of the corner of her eye: a boy with shaggy black hair, wearing weather-stained leather, apparently looking in a shop window. Suddenly his head came around and he gazed full at her, and she stumbled on the cobblestones.

Ramon caught her with a solicitous hand on her arm. "Are you all right?"

"Fine," she said a little breathlessly. She didn't look back again, but she didn't need to.

The boy had been Kalar.

He's not dead! was her first glad thought, but anger followed. *He hated me. He should have been glad to be rid of me. Why is he here?* She almost pointed him out to the prince, but something stopped her. Kalar had saved her on the Crag, after all; and with his background, the prince and his father might think he was connected with the "dangerous elements" Ar-Naathon had mentioned. *Let him be,* she thought. *He can follow me all he wants. As long as he doesn't cause any trouble...*

Ahead, the street opened out into another courtyard, this one empty of merchants, though wagons and people crisscrossed its large square paving blocks. Amarynth glimpsed a high white wall. "The Temple of the One," said the prince, and a moment later they emerged into the open and she could see it all clearly.

Fully as big as the palace, it stood foursquare, with a tall, slender tower at each corner, tapering gracefully to needle-sharp spires from which flew long banners of red, blue, gold, and white. At its centre, a dome of marble, plated with bronze, shone like a second sun. Atop it, contained within a bronze basin, a clear yellow flame burned, whipped by the wind but never going out.

Its beauty astonished Amarynth, and though she still thought it unnecessary and foolish to build such a place to worship the One who was everywhere, its magnificence moved her.

It loomed ever-larger as they neared it, the dome gradually disappearing behind the white wall. They mounted the two-dozen steps that led to its mirror-like silver doors, which stood open; but just before they passed into the dimness beyond Amarynth glanced back.

Kalar stood at the courtyard's edge, watching her.

Inside, a long, high-ceilinged passageway opened abruptly into the main chamber of the temple, the vast room beneath the dome. A hundred oil lamps, hung by silver chains from the soaring roof, reflected from the burnished bronze of the dome's interior, filling the air with a soft yellow glow.

Centred beneath the dome a single flame, the symbol of the One, burned atop a crystal pillar, an echo of the greater flame atop the temple roof. Around that pillar people stood or knelt, gazing deeply into the flame, praying or meditating.

The rest of the vast space was empty. The floor of

black marble, inset with silver stars, might have been the void of space itself.

Amarynth gazed around in wonder, but Ramon gave her only a moment to stare before tugging her along the edge of the chamber to a small door. Beyond lay a narrow corridor of plain white marble, punctuated by more doors. "The Temple Wanderers live here," Ramon said as he led the way down it. "There are more than a hundred of them."

"Did all the city's Singers become Wanderers?" asked Amarynth, seeking some reassurance that what she was about to do was something of which her grandfather would have approved.

Ramon sighed. "Not all could accept the new power. It was very sad. Some of the greatest gave up their calling."

"What happened to them?"

But Ramon, opening a door, seemed not to hear her. *All questions in their proper time*, she thought as she followed him through it. *It's beginning to seem the proper time will never come.*

The room beyond, small, square, and plain, held a desk of black wood, bearing only a red quill pen thrust into an ink bottle, two chairs, and ceiling-high shelves filled with books along three walls. The smell of their leather bindings instantly brought to Amarynth's mind her grandfather's library, where he had searched in vain for some clue as to the nature of the Beast.

Behind the desk sat a man in the black robe of a

Wanderer. "I've brought Spirit Singer Amarynth, Wanderer Thesman," said Ramon.

"Thank you, Your Highness." As Amarynth entered, Thesman stood and motioned her to a chair. She took it, studying him.

He was of indeterminate middle age, with greying hair cut short and a lined, pale face. His lips were thin and drawn and his nose had a distinct hook to it. Blue eyes glittered beneath thin black brows, which arched suddenly. "Do you approve?"

Amarynth blushed. "I'm sorry."

"Quite all right." Thesman looked at the prince, who nodded and went out, closing the door behind him. Then Thesman sat down again. "The ceremony is even now being prepared, in one of our Spirit Chambers," he said. "But I understand you have some questions."

At last! Amarynth thought, and, leaning forward, poured out what had happened to her grandfather, why she had been sent to the mountains, and what had happened when she tried to Sing Timara. "What is this Beast?" she finished. "You have to tell me! Otherwise—I don't know if I can go into the Between World again."

Thesman pursed his lips. "Your grandfather's fear was unfortunate," he said. "It caused his downfall. Had we known there was a village, and therefore a Spirit Singer, in so remote a place, we would have sent a Wanderer sooner...but, well, what's done is done."

"What do you mean, his fear caused his downfall?"

Amarynth said, voice trembling. "The Beast killed him! It's as simple as that."

"Not at all," said Thesman. He smiled and spread his hands. "The Beast is the source of our power."

Amarynth hardly heard the crash of her chair against the floor as she stumbled to her feet in horror.

CHAPTER 13

"Sit down," Thesman said mildly; when Amarynth made no move to comply, he said it again, sharper.

She picked up her chair and did as she was told, but on the edge of the seat. "How can that monstrosity be the source of your power?" she demanded. "Are you as evil as it is?"

"But my dear young *apprentice* Spirit Singer," said the Wanderer, "who said it is evil?"

"I've seen it!"

"So have I. My interpretation, and that of Ar-Naathon, and the hundred Wanderers here in this temple, and the scores of others outside in the wide world, is different. Would you care to hear it?"

"How can there be any *interpretation* of something so obvious?"

"The Between World is not a place of hard and certain facts—you know that," said Thesman reasonably.

"What you see there depends very much on what is within you. That is why we Spirit Singers have always led rather ascetic lives, denying ourselves this and that, contemplating and meditating all the time. We must be serene, or our own turmoil will spill over into the Between World, which can lead to truly terrifying experiences."

Amarynth unwillingly remembered her own vision of her dead grandfather. "I know that. But this Beast—"

"—is no beast at all, except to your fearful inner vision. Your grandfather was having bad dreams; why, I cannot say. We all have such dreams at times. He was old; he confused his dreams with reality. Thus he was fearful of entering the Between World, and when this—Power— became apparent to him—as it had to, eventually, for it is drawn to all Spirit Singers—he interpreted it as a monster threatening to swallow him whole, rather than as a source of energy he could tap. He fought the incipient Link with that Power, and the strain killed him. Had he only accepted it, he would have become a Wanderer then and there, freed from the constraints that have limited Spirit Singers through the centuries."

Thesman leaned forward as he continued. "Not surprisingly, his reaction and subsequent death also poisoned your mind against the Power—you saw it the same way he did. Had *you* accepted it, *you* would already be a Wanderer—and Timara would not wander the Between World." He sat back again, shaking his head sadly. "Or, had you simply left the child in the path of the

Power, it would have taken her, and she would not be the terrified nomad spirit she now is."

"But where did this Power come from?" Amarynth said. "How come my grandfather had never seen or heard of it before?" She looked at the high bookshelves surrounding them, at the book-spines of red and brown and black leather, aglitter here and there with gold lettering. "He consulted all his books, and could find nothing..."

"I doubt," said Thesman drily, following her gaze, "that your grandfather's library was the equal of that of the temple—what you see here is a mere fraction of it. It was in some of the most ancient tomes of all, books and scrolls untouched since the Landing, that Ar-Naathon found the key to the Power." He reached out and ran his finger along the edge of the red quill pen. "It is not a new thing, you know. It is ancient. The Old Ones, in the land across the sea—they had access to it. But it fell into disuse as their descendants dwindled, cut off from the knowledge and glory of that old world." Amarynth watched his finger, caressing first one side of the feather, then the other. He seemed almost to have forgotten she was there. "Now we can begin anew," he murmured. "We can reclaim the power of the Old Ones, and someday their land, as well..."

He blinked suddenly and pulled his hand back. "Well. At least now we know what we must watch for during today's ceremony. Don't worry, child, we can ease your fear enough so that you can accept the Power. Within the hour, you'll be a Wanderer, too—and ready to return to your village. Come." He stood, and, bemused and uneasy, Amarynth followed him out into the white corridor. Ramon was gone, but two middle-aged Wanderers and two Black Guards waited. She stared at them, then turned to Thesman.

"Am I a prisoner?" she demanded.

He raised one eyebrow. "What an odd question. Of course not, child. These men are part of the ceremony. This way." He led her down the hall to a door of black wood, adorned with gilded, intricately carved branches and leaves, golden apples nestled among them. Despite Thesman's assurance, Amarynth was very much aware of the presence of the Black Guards behind her, and her unease grew. The whole atmosphere was wrong— nothing like her lone journey to the Gate to become a Spirit Singer she would have made under her grandfather's supervision. This was like—like some kind of barbaric sacrificial ceremony of ancient days.

The room beyond the carved door only strengthened that impression. Domed and round, a small copy of the temple's great central chamber, its walls were swathed in thick, black cloth that muffled every sound. Within that cocoon, the blood-warm air hung utterly still.

A single candle burned at the chamber's centre. At Thesman's direction, the three Wanderers and Amarynth formed a circle around that unwavering flame. The Black Guards stationed themselves on either side of the door, and though nothing could be seen of their eyes behind their helmet visors, Amarynth felt certain they were watching her. "May the One guide us," intoned Thesman; then said, "Centre, friends."

Amarynth felt cold despite the stagnant air. "I don't —" she began, but suddenly felt an outside touch forcing her concentration inward, preparing her to enter the Between World whether she wished it or not. She gasped, appalled that such a thing was even possible, but already it was done.

"We begin," Thesman said.

The chamber faded into a transparent shell, and the four of them stood, shadowy figures enclosing burning light, upon the grey plain of the Between World. Around them stretched the city of Havenheart, like a model made of glass; here and there other Wanderers burned like distant torches, and rising everywhere were the silvery traces of Paths. Amarynth looked around in astonishment. She would never have thought the Between World could seem crowded.

Over all hung darkness, and a sense of oppression, like the almost tangible weight of an approaching thunderstorm in the Lower World. "Do you feel the Power?" asked Thesman.

"Yes," whispered Amarynth; not adding that, more than ever, she sensed it as evil.

Yet the Wanderer somehow knew her thought. "You are frightened," he said. "Your perception is still tainted. But if you are strong, all will be well." He looked up. "Here is our Path."

Abruptly Amarynth's perception changed and they stood on a Path that had not been there an instant before, centred over the Spirit Chamber. "So quickly—" she said, startled.

"With the Power, many things are possible." Already they were speeding toward the darkness, through the spider-like web of interconnecting Paths—and Amarynth heard a distant cry, growing rapidly nearer.

Suddenly Timara appeared, a tiny flicker of soul-light that clung to her, all shadow of her long-departed body gone. Thesman looked back. "With the Power, you will be able to rid yourself of that unfortunate spirit."

Amarynth murmured comfort to the tiny, frightened soul, and to herself. "Soon," she whispered. "Very soon."

"Soon indeed," said Thesman. "We approach the Power."

Amarynth looked up. All the Paths came together in a single broad way that disappeared into looming darkness. Timara whimpered. "What do I do?" Amarynth asked.

"Only submit," said Thesman. "The Power does the rest. It will take you and change you. You will become like us. A Wanderer."

"Like us," the other two whispered. They rushed ahead of her, spreading their arms to embrace the onrushing blackness. "Fill us!" they chanted with Thesman. "Fill us, O Power! Fill us!"

For a moment Amarynth saw the darkness as they did —a place of warmth and comfort, a place without thought, without fear, without any of the emotions that roiled human minds; a place where many became one, serving a great purpose, shorn of doubt, released from the responsibility of free will. For that one moment she, too, stretched out her arms to the Power—

And then Timara screamed, a tiny, agonized sound, and her terror of the darkness echoed in Amarynth. For an instant she escaped the subtle coercion from the Wanderers, coercion she had hardly felt, and saw the Power again as she had always seen it before—as a horrible, formless Beast, a thinking, evil creature bending men to its own will.

Timara's spirit struggled wildly, trying to escape; but the bond with Amarynth held her, and Amarynth in turn was held by the Wanderers. Except—they were almost fully lost in the Power, and for a moment, had forgotten her.

With a wrench that tore through her like lightning, she broke free. She saw Thesman and the others turn toward her, and behind them the Beast roared, and swelled up over her like a great wave—but already she was fleeing, back along the Path, back to where the single way split into hundreds, back toward the shadowy form of the Spirit Chamber. Once again she flung Timara away, clear of the onrushing evil that followed her, once again she heard the child's heart-rending cry—then she crashed into the plain of the Lower World and suddenly fell to her knees in the Spirit Chamber.

An instant later the Wanderers' statue-like bodies,

too, came to life. Thesman broke from his place in the circle, seized her arm in a pincer-like grip, and jerked her, hard, to her feet. "You little fool!" he snarled. "But so be it. You're not the first Singer to refuse the Power. Now it's up to Ar-Naathon to decide what to do with you. Guards!" The Black Guards stepped forward in unison, and Thesman propelled her toward them. "Take her to the master!"

"Where's Prince Ramon?" Amarynth cried.

"Ka-Raamon can do nothing for you now," Thesman spat. "You won't see him again. Guards, go!"

Held in strong, mailed hands, Amarynth was taken from the Spirit Chamber, back down the hallway into the great domed room, and from there into the sun-drenched square outside. She looked wildly around, but Kalar, too, had vanished, and none of the people in the square would even meet the eyes of one so obviously a prisoner of the Black Guards. "Help me!" she cried to a man leading a roan therra, but he turned his face and hurried off with the beast, and the Black Guard on her right pulled her toward him and struck the back of her head so hard her ears rang and she staggered.

They took her back into the street she and Ramon had followed from the palace, and she stumbled along, held too tightly even to struggle, head aching, every dark suspicion having been proven right.

Halfway down the street an alley opened to the left. As Amarynth and her two guards passed it, six men burst from its shadows, swords drawn. The Black Guards flung

Amarynth to the ground and seized their own blades but were overwhelmed and cut down before Amarynth could even regain her feet. Passersby screamed and ran. In an instant the street was deserted, save for the mysterious attackers and the dead Black Guards. Amarynth stared, horrified, at blood puddling on the cobblestones, then someone clutched her arm and she screamed and struck out blindly.

Her hand bounced off Kalar's forearm. He seized her wrist and pulled her into the alley from which the attackers had emerged and into which they had already fled. After a few yards he ducked left into a side passage, then led her down more crazily twisting alleys and lanes for several minutes before suddenly thrusting her into an overhung passageway, stinking sickly-sweet of garbage, dark as a tomb despite the sun outside.

"Are we safe?" she asked breathlessly, then gasped as Kalar shoved her hard against the wet stones and snatched from his belt his long, black-hilted dagger.

CHAPTER 14

As Amarynth stood petrified, the sharp stones of the wall pressing painfully into her back, Kalar grabbed the chain that held her Emblem and jerked the smooth black stone toward him. It was as dead and lifeless as ever. He stared at it, then withdrew his knife and let the Emblem drop.

White and shaking, she slapped her hands to his chest and shoved him away so hard he staggered. "Get away from me!" she shouted.

"You were taken into the temple to be made into a Wanderer, weren't you?" he snapped at her as he straightened. "I had to make sure you aren't one."

"They brought me out of the temple a prisoner. Wasn't that proof enough?"

"For all I knew it was an honour guard." He sheathed his dagger and glanced back the way they had come. "Now, are we going to stand here arguing all day? Men-at-arms or more Black Guards will be searching these streets any minute."

Amarynth clenched her fist around her Emblem. "Where now?"

Kalar jerked his head toward a narrow street to their right. He led her down worn cobblestones until they ended in mud, the plaster and brick buildings of the city's centre gave way to sagging wooden shacks, and the only people in sight were emaciated creatures slinking from doorway to doorway as though shunning the daylight. The stench of garbage and sewage grew until it was all Amarynth could do to keep from gagging, but Kalar didn't seem to notice it.

Ahead something glittered, and Amarynth realized they were approaching the bank of the Lifeblood. The ruins of a once-fine house slumped alongside the water like the skeleton of some great creature, and Kalar, after a careful look around to be sure they weren't being watched, led her to a sagging gate in the crumbling wall surrounding the structure, almost hidden beneath a massive vilio tree, so overgrown its trailing tendrils brushed the ground.

The gate in the shadow of that tree opened onto a path canopied by trellised gazelda flowers gone wild, forming a dim green corridor heavy with the sugary scent of the drooping yellow blooms. Parts of the gazelda bushes extended well inside the rotting trellis, so that Amarynth had to duck more than once to avoid tangling her hair in the thorny branches.

At the end of the passage an open door led into the dim interior of the house, but Kalar ignored it, instead squeezing between the end of the trellis and the wall. Amarynth followed, and found herself in another narrow passage, formed by the house on her right and a tall green hedge on her left. It led to a small building nestled up against the house but not joined to it, most likely a gardener's shed at one time.

Kalar opened the wooden door and motioned her through, then stepped in behind her, closing the door behind them. Amarynth looked around at empty shelves and shuttered windows, then down at Kalar, who had fallen to his knees. He rapped on the wooden floor in a complex rhythm. He paused, then repeated the cadence, and Amarynth started as the rap was repeated from below. An instant later she heard the sound of bolts being drawn, and then a section of the floor heaved up. Kalar seized it and set it to one side. Bright eyes peered at Amarynth from either side of the nose guard of a battered helmet. "This her?" said a gruff voice.

"Who else?" said Kalar.

The other man laughed. "Fair enough." He ducked out of sight again, but his voice came back to them. "Come on, then. Herkas is waiting."

Kalar looked up at Amarynth and pointed to the hole in the floor. "You first."

Cautiously she peered over the edge. A flimsy wooden ladder descended to a paved floor fifteen feet below, lit by a sputtering torch. The armed man who had greeted them had pulled off his helmet, revealing a balding pate. He grinned up at her. "Sometime today would be agreeable!"

Amarynth turned and found an alarmingly shaky rung with her foot. Moments later, she stepped rather breathlessly off the ladder into a corridor that ended abruptly to her left but to her right gave way to stairs descending even deeper into the earth. A musty smell rolled up from below. "Watch your head," said the bald man, and Amarynth quickly moved out of the way of Kalar's booted feet.

Kalar paused to reseat the door in the floor above, and shoot home the four bolts, one on each side, that held it there. Then he descended the ladder. Once he was down, the bald man pointed at the stairs. "Herkas is in the council chamber," he told Kalar.

Kalar nodded his thanks, took Amarynth's arm, and started down. Amarynth glanced back to see the bald man laying the rickety ladder against the wall.

She turned back to Kalar. "Who is Herkas?" she demanded as they descended. "And what is this place?"

"You'll find out soon enough," Kalar said without looking at her.

Amarynth stopped on the steps and jerked her arm free of his grasp. "I've had enough of waiting for answers! That's what landed me in the temple. Tell me where we're going and why, or I don't take another step!"

Kalar folded his arms and gave her a sour look. "You

can't spend the rest of your life on these stairs, and Yafel up there won't let you go back."

"We'll see about that!" Amarynth turned and started climbing.

Kalar lunged after her, caught her arm, and jerked her around to face him. "If you leave here now Ar-Naathon or Ka-Raamon will have you before sunset!"

"Ramon may be just the one I should go to!"

"By the One, I rescued you!" Kalar exploded. "Don't tell me you still trust that so-called prince. You fled his precious temple—"

"What does the prince know about what goes on there? He's not a Spirit Singer. He may have had nothing to do with it." Amarynth started up again, only to be stopped by Kalar once more.

"I can't let you leave!"

"Why?" Amarynth turned on him, furious. "So you rescued me. Believe me, I thank you for it—but I don't understand it. Why didn't you stay in your mountains? You told me there you were finished with me!"

Kalar met her angry eyes with his own for a long moment, then suddenly released her arm. "All right!" He thrust a finger at the stairs. "Sit down and I'll tell you what happened. Then we'll go see Herkas!"

"Maybe." But Amarynth sat.

Kalar folded his arms again and leaned back against the wall, staring at his boots. "I never should have slept that night," he said. "But I didn't really believe the Black Guards were after you—or that they could find my hiding place. I woke when that Black Guard crashed into the room. I remember jumping to my feet—and the next thing I knew it was morning, you were gone, there was blood all over my face and my head felt like someone had lit a fire inside.

"I followed the Black Guard's tracks, and yours, what there were of them, down to the main road, where they joined wagon and therra-tracks, fresh ones, heading out of the mountains—toward Havenheart. I kept following, on foot, at first, though I remedied that at the first village I came to." He gave her a fierce look. "Ar-Naathon and his Wanderers can't control everyone, even with the fear of dying unSung. Oppression breeds opposition. There are those in Haven who are resisting. They gave me a therra and sent messages on ahead of me by carrier-bird.

"I shadowed you for your entire journey, seeking an opportunity to free you—but it never came. The Black Guards were always watchful.

"When we came to the city, you entered through the main gate and I entered by a more secret way. I reported to Herkas, who leads those who still stand against Ar-Naathon. His spies in the palace had told him you would be taken to the temple today and made a Wanderer.

"We meant to rescue you before you ever reached the temple, but you appeared earlier than we expected. Our men weren't in place. We had to wait until you emerged —and the rest you know." He straightened. "Now, Herkas is waiting..."

Amarynth didn't move. "The rest I do *not* know!

You've told me *what* you did, but not *why*. You told me you hated all Spirit Singers. Yet you've risked your life to follow me here. Tell me why!"

Kalar gave her a scornful look. "Surely you can figure it out. You were my guest, as you so pointedly reminded me when you needed my help. You were taken while under my protection—and the safety of a guest is sacred."

"Sacred? I though you considered nothing sacred. The importance of hospitality comes from the Master, Kalar, did you know that? 'We all make many journeys in our lives before we make the final one in death,'" she quoted from *The Master's Path*. "'When such a journey brings a stranger to your door, honour him, and treat him as you would wish to be treated in like circumstance.' Your sacred duty was given you by a Spirit Singer!"

"My duty as Guesthost is sacred because my father died for it," Kalar retorted. "I care nothing for what you Death Squawkers claim. I had to rescue you or dishonour my father's memory." He pointed down the stairs. "*Now* will you come with me to Herkas?"

Amarynth rose. "I doubt most Guesthosts would have found sufficient reason in their vows to come after someone taken by the Black Guard," she flung at him.

"My father would have," Kalar said shortly.

They descended the stairs in silence, but as they started down a dark, dank corridor, walled, floored, and roofed with irregular, head-sized blocks of black stone, Amarynth said, "You still haven't told me where we are."

"This is the redoubt of those fighting Ar-Naathon," said Kalar. He pulled her against the wall to allow two armed men to hurry past, barely sparing them a glance. "The owner of the house above us, long years past, was a smuggler of some repute...and success, as you can tell from the size of the place. Certain of Herkas's followers happened to know of these tunnels, while Ar-Naathon, fortunately, does not."

"Most fortunately," said Amarynth. She remembered Ar-Naathon telling her that the Wanderer Elsdar had had ties with "evil men" who would have murdered her had the prince not met her at the gate. She glanced at Kalar's hard face. *He would never work with friends of the Wanderer who had killed his father*, she thought. *Like everything else Ar-Naathon told me, that was a lie.*

And Prince Ramon? When she had first met him, she had thought she might have found a friend. That morning she had suspected him of being false. Both times, he seemed to have been playing a role. Yet she had liked him—had enjoyed walking with him through Havenheart, enjoyed his banter and good humour. Somewhere beneath whatever falsity he had shown her, she thought the friend she had sensed might really exist.

Was it really possible, as she had said to Kalar, that Ramon had not known what awaited her in the temple?

Yes, she decided. *He is not a Spirit Singer or Wanderer. He hasn't been touched by the Beast. And he lives a sheltered life here in the city. Maybe he doesn't know the truth about his father or the Wanderers or the Black Guards.*

Though it seemed unlikely she would ever see Prince Ka-Raamon again, she hoped that was true.

They passed other halls and anonymous wooden doors, then Kalar abruptly turned left and led her down a short, wider passageway to dark double doors that swung open as he approached. Two armed men with drawn swords barred their way, but stood aside as a deep voice said, "Let them pass."

The room beyond was as big as the great hall in the tower at Covedrift, though here there were no coloured windows, only smoky brass lamps hung on cords from the vaulted ceiling. Around a black oval table at the room's centre sat five men. They stood as Kalar and Amarynth entered.

Kalar stopped so abruptly Amarynth trod on his heels, then had to step around him to see what had brought the sudden, granite stiffness to his face and bearing.

At the table's head was a man who had to be Herkas, clad in simple brown homespun and leather as weather-stained as Kalar's. A naked broadsword lay on the table before him. His black hair was salted with grey, and his lined face bore the look of one who had seen and done much that haunted him.

But the other four were dressed as Amarynth was—except their robes were white, and the Emblems on their chests blazed with the deep purple light that her grandfather's had always shown. *True Spirit Singers at last!*

"What does Herkas need with such as these?" Kalar demanded.

The Spirit Singers, all of an age with Amarynth's grandfather, exchanged silent glances. Reply was left to Herkas, whose mild tone overlaid a hint of steel. "Ar-Naathon's power comes from the spirit world," he said. "We can fight his men-at-arms and even the foul Black Guards blade to blade, but we cannot fight what we cannot see." He spread his hands. "These men can."

"These—men—like the rest of their kind, will weaken your will and turn you over to Ar-Naathon!" Kalar almost spat the words. "All Death Squawkers are alike, whether they wear white or black!"

Amarynth turned toward him with rising anger, but Herkas spoke first.

"I command here," he said, and now the steel in his voice was laid as bare as that of the blade on the table. "Who are you to question me, *boy*? Maybe you have good reason to fear Spirit Singers—there are those who do, though I would have thought you too young to have accumulated such blackness on your soul." Kalar's eyes widened, but Herkas did not relent. "The Singers are our allies. If you cannot bear that thought, then leave us."

Kalar's jaw clenched, but he said nothing more.

Herkas stared at him a full minute longer, then turned to Amarynth. "We have been expecting you," he said, his voice gentle once more.

She bowed slightly. "Commander Herkas. Brothers."

The eldest of the Singers smiled and motioned her to

a seat. "Come, little sister! We must talk."

Kalar spun and stalked out of the room, but as Amarynth half-turned, Herkas said, "Let him go." She heard pain in his voice and turned back to him questioningly. "I know he blames a Spirit Singer for his father's death," he said tiredly. "Of course he hates them. But he hates Ar-Naathon more. He's a good lad, though a bit hot-headed. He'll return."

"I am Mythos," the old Spirit Singer interjected, as though anxious to get on to more important matters. "You are Amarynth?"

"Yes." She sat in the proffered chair and took a deep breath. "I think I should tell you first that Ar-Naathon says he can sense me. He'll track me here. I should go—"

"You're safe here," said another Singer. "Ar-Naathon, through his black Power, can indeed sense true Singers—but there are limits." He gestured at the stone ceiling. "There are many feet of rock between us and the surface, and this room lies beneath the river. Flowing water is a powerful barrier. We do not believe even Ar-Naathon can pierce all that."

"You don't believe?" Amarynth said. "Aren't you *sure*?"

"No," Mythos said quietly. "We cannot be sure of anything where Ar-Naathon is concerned. But we believe we are safe here because he has never come after us." He shook his head. "We should be up above. So many people are dying unSung—or worse, Sung by the Wanderers—Sung to feed the Beast."

Amarynth felt cold. "To *feed* the Beast?"

Mythos nodded.

"What is the Beast?"

"You have seen it."

"Yes, but—"

"Then you know as much as we. Where it came from, and why, we do not know. All we know is that Ar-Naathon—Nathon, he was then, just a simple Singer of the Temple—found some reference to it in an ancient text and called it to him in the Between World. At first it was only one more small, dark, lost creature haunting the Path—but unlike the others, who have no real power, this one grew. And grew. We didn't know how, then, but we do now." He shuddered. "Ar-Naathon was feeding it—feeding it with the spirits he was Singing, delivering them not to the Gate but to the hungry maw of that monstrous being. In return, it gave him powers such as no other Spirit Singer had ever had: power to sense other Singers, power to build a Path from nothing, anywhere, anytime —though a Path that leads only to the Beast, not to the Gate—and power to Link other Singers to the Beast, making them into shadows of himself."

"Wanderers," Amarynth whispered, feeling sick.

"Wanderers," Mythos confirmed. "Whatever those men were like originally, if they accept that Link—and the lure of power is strong temptation to even the best of men—they become slaves to the Beast, existing only to feed it more souls and to serve the ends of Ar-Naathon."

Amarynth's fingers ached from gripping the arms of her chair. "What about the Black Guards?"

"We don't know what they are. But they are utterly submissive to the will of Ar-Naathon and the Wanderers."

"He must be stopped!" Amarynth cried. "It's—it's monstrous!" She looked from face to face. "There are four of you! There must be other true Singers left. Surely together you can—"

"Singly or together, it makes no difference," said Mythos. "We tried, many times, when Ar-Naathon was far less powerful than he is now—and failed. We dare not try again, for fear we will inadvertently reveal this place to him."

"Then he must be killed!" Amarynth burst out, then swallowed, remembering she was a Spirit Singer. "I'm sorry. That wasn't—"

Herkas laughed harshly. "The Singers would not attempt it. But the rest of us have no such compunction. We have tried often...and we, too, always fail. The Power Ar-Naathon serves protects him not only in the spirit world, but in this one."

"Then is all lost?"

"We have one hope left," Mythos replied; and Amarynth, looking around the table, saw that all heads had turned toward her.

CHAPTER 15

"I don't understand," Amarynth said, staring back at them all. "What hope?"

"We have received a message," said Mythos. "A very strange message; but one that may hold promise."

"A message from whom?"

"We don't know." The answer came from another of the Singers. "We know nothing about who sent it or why."

Mythos silence him with a glance that spoke of a long quarrel still unresolved. "The message is from a Sprit Singer; we know that much," he said, turning back to Amarynth. "And a Singer of great strength, for he sent his message through one of the servants of Ar-Naathon."

"A Wanderer?"

"Precisely. Ten days ago, a Wanderer was found in the shed that hides the entrance. When discovered, he demanded to see me. Brought before me, he spat out this message as though it burned him, then collapsed unconscious. Herkas's men took him then." Mythos turned a reproachful look on the commander. "We thought they would kill him, despite our protests—"

"And we would have, too," said Herkas, unperturbed. "Except when he awoke he had no memory of where he had been or even who he was. We set him free, though of course we watched him. He did not return to the temple. He left the city and we have not seen him since."

"That was proof enough of this mysterious Singer's power," Mythos continued, "and inclined us to take his message seriously." He closed his eyes and recited, "'The Beast rises again, its strength reborn and waxing. If its power is not broken, it will devour two worlds. Send me a Singer who has not Sung, before two-score days have passed. It is the only hope.'" He opened his eyes.

Amarynth blinked. "A Singer who has not Sung? But...why me? Why not one of your own apprentices?"

"We have none," said another of the Singers. "All were taken, and either slain or made Wanderers themselves."

"We did not know about you when we received the message, though we thought some with the Gift might still survive untouched by Ar-Naathon in the most distant reaches of Haven," said Mythos. "We were at a loss; two-score days was not enough time to seek them out—"

"Then Kalar arrived and told us of you," Herkas finished.

"I can't defeat the Beast!" cried Amarynth. "I dare not even face it again! Twice it has almost had me!"

"Perhaps you won't *have* to face it," said Mythos. "We don't know what this strange Singer intends; perhaps he will battle the Beast himself but requires your help. The message does not say."

"The message doesn't say anything! It could be a trick of Ar-Naathon's."

"Exactly what I've been—" began the dissenting Singer.

"If it is a trick, then all hope is lost," Mythos said sharply to both of them. Then his tone softened. "Amarynth, we cannot force you to go to this man. If you refuse, we'll search for someone else, and you are still free to remain in the safety of this place...though how long that safety will last, I cannot say. But I plead with you—I beg you—accept. The Beast grows stronger every day, and soon it will be too late, even for this slim chance."

Amarynth sat silent, staring at her hands, folded before her on the table. In her mind she saw her grandfather laughing in the sunshine, his white hair astir in the sea breeze; saw the people of Covedrift dancing around the beacon fires as they celebrated a successful fishing season; saw Davin smiling shyly at her; saw Potras and Elenor pleading with her to help their daughter...and heard the cry of Timara, still lost between the worlds. Wanderers and Black Guards crowded into the images, more and more of them, until they merged into the black horror that threatened all of Haven.

She had promised herself she would never again go against her deepest feelings the way she had when she had allowed herself to be taken to the temple. She had known it was wrong, that it was against everything she had learned and believed in, but she had let herself be swayed by Ar-Naathon's fine words and the prince's friendliness.

That friendliness had been the greatest temptation. How often, back in Covedrift, had she hated being different, longed to be treated just like everyone else? The prince had given her that, heartfelt or not, and she wished she could thank him for it.

Now she was being set apart again, even more than by her Gift—except this, unlike her Gift, she could refuse.

Reason told her that was the route to follow, that to go to the unknown man who had sent the mysterious message was foolhardiness that could get her killed. But this time her heart urged her on, instead of calling her back.

The men at this table were true Spirit Singers, like her grandfather, not pawns of the Beast. They might be last true Singers left in Haven. If there were ever to be more, the Beast had to be destroyed. If what they asked of her, hopeless though it seemed, truly was the last hope, how could she refuse?

She clenched her fists. "All right," she said. "I'll go."

The tension in the room eased perceptibly. Mythos took a deep breath. "Thank you," he said. "We have set aside supplies for you, and a guide to take you from the city and set you on the right road. After that—"

"After that, I will be with her," said Kalar's voice from behind Amarynth.

She twisted around in her chair: he stood in the doorway, scowling. "*What?*"

"I said I'm going with you," he growled.

"Why?" she demanded. "You rescued me. I am no longer your guest, so your 'sacred duty' is done. You owe me nothing. And you would be accompanying a Spirit Singer—a 'Death Squawker'—on a journey to another Singer."

"I let you be taken by the Black Guard," Kalar said. "I won't let it happen again. Until you are free of that threat, my duty continues. You are still under my protection."

Amarynth opened her mouth to argue that if that were true, every Guesthost who had ever burned someone's meat would be bound to follow him or her around to make sure it was cooked properly thereafter—but then closed it again without speaking. Even Kalar's company would be better than none at all, she decided, especially on the road to...

I don't even know where I'm going, she realized. She turned back to Mythos. "Where is the Singer?"

"Icethorn Peak."

"I know the Mountains of the North well," Kalar said. He came to stand beside her. "There is no peak named Icethorn."

"It does not lie in the Northern Range."

Kalar stiffened. Amarynth glanced at him, then at Mythos. "Then where—" she began, but go no further, realizing suddenly what the Singer meant.

Mythos met her gaze firmly. "The Haunted Mountains."

She paled. "A Singer? There?"

"So said the message." Mythos gave her a hard look. "Does that change your decision?"

Amarynth started to say yes, it most certainly did— but paused. *There is no safe road I can take, not with Ar-Naathon after me.* "No," she said at last.

Mythos looked from her to Kalar. "And what about you?" he said. "No one has asked you to follow this path."

"I do not believe in ghosts," he said. "Any more than I believe in Spirit Singers. And mountains I grew up with. I'm going."

Mythos nodded, then glanced at a white time-candle on a sideboard. "It approaches noon," he said. "We'll send you on your way at dark. In the meantime, I suggest you eat, and sleep."

In a small chamber half an hour later, after a meal of coarse bread and stringy meat, and having exchanged the Wanderer's robe for her own white tunic and sky-blue leggings (for, to Amarynth's delight, Kalar had brought her pack with him all the way from his hut above the Cragway, including her beloved cloak with the seashell brooch and, best of all, her own comfortable boots),

Amarynth lay on a hard cot and stared at the cracked plaster of the wall. Sleep was undoubtedly a good idea before an all-night sojourn, but it seemed as impossibly far away as Covedrift.

There had been no Singer in her home village for almost three weeks. What would the elders think had become of her? How long would the people stay, with the tower unoccupied and the Spirit Chamber cold and dark?

Or...

She squeezed her eyes tight shut. Or would a Wanderer have reached even that desolate shore by this time?

That's another reason I must go on this strange mission, she thought fiercely. *I promised to return with a Singer for Covedrift, and that can never happen while the Beast is in the Between World. For Covedrift, for my grandfather, for Timara—for myself!—I have to go.*

Yet determination did nothing to lessen the fear. The Beast devoured souls, Mythos had told her. Timara so far was free, but what of Davin? What of her grandfather? And if she faced the Beast again—what of her?

Eventually Amarynth dozed, to be wakened abruptly and unpleasantly from dark dreams by the door crashing open. She jerked upright on the cot and stared at a man in rusty mail and patched blue surcoat, a battered, naked sword in his hand and a dented steel cap on his head. "Ar-Naathon's men are attacking!" he cried. "Herkas says you have to leave *now!*"

Amarynth snatched her prepared backpack from the floor by the bed and stuffed her feet into her boots, while the man stared up and down the corridor. Faintly Amarynth heard shouts and the clash of steel.

Those sounds became clearer when she emerged into the hallway, just as Kalar burst from his room next door, a sword in one hand and his own black-hilted dagger in the other. "They've broken through two entrances," the man in the blue surcoat said breathlessly. He dashed down the corridor, Kalar and Amarynth close behind. "Pray they haven't found the one outside the wall!"

The hall met another at right angles. Their guide burst into the intersection ahead of them, turned right—and fell, black feathers protruding from his back.

Amarynth bit off a scream as Kalar flung out his arm and slammed her back against the wall. Footsteps clattered toward them, slowing as they neared the corner. Amarynth heard the sound of a crossbow being cocked, and shrank against the stone as Kalar crept forward, beads of sweat on his forehead glinting gold in the torchlight.

The shouts and screams of battle grew nearer—and suddenly the man with the crossbow, not a Black Guard, as Amarynth had expected, but one of Ar-Naathon's men-at-arms, leaped into view.

Kalar's sword smashed the crossbow, and before the soldier could even cry out, found his throat. Blood fountained and he dropped to the ground, choking and twitching before falling still.

Amarynth staggered back against the wall, bent over, hands on her knees, and threw up. She stayed there, spitting, sick to her soul as well as her stomach. Two dead men here—who knew how many elsewhere in the warren—they had to be Sung! But there was nothing she could do, nothing anyone could do while the Beast lurked in the Between World. The Wanderers would come, would feed these souls like so many others to that monstrous creature—the horror of it almost blinded her. *The Beast gorges on war!* she realized. *War, murder, violence...it feasts on it!* Herkas's counter-revolution—even if it succeeded, even if he drove off today's attackers and regrouped somewhere else—still served Ar-Naathon. Every battle, every death, added to the Beast's power, strengthening the Master of the City rather than weakening him.

Kalar hauled her upright. "Be as sick as you want— later," he shouted. "For now, run!"

She stumbled after him, down the corridor their guard had started to take. "Do you know where the exit is?" she choked out.

"No," Kalar said grimly. "But we're headed in the right direction. Just hope there are no more intersections."

There weren't. The corridor deteriorated, from smooth-cut stone to rough rock to timbered earth and finally to packed dirt, which in places had collapsed into soft, muddy piles they had to clamber over. Amarynth felt the weight of the ground pressing down on her as she had not in the well-made tunnels of the warren's centre.

The tunnel ended. Five feet above them leaf-green light streamed through an opening. Rough footholds in the earth led up to it; Kalar sheathed his sword and scrambled up, then turned and pulled Amarynth up after him.

She emerged into a cramped dome woven of branches, over which grew vines with broad, thick leaves. An opening led out of the dome, just big enough to wriggle through; Amarynth did so, face-down in the dirt, then stood, brushing at the mud on the front of her tunic.

"It's about time," said a dry voice behind her. "I've been expecting you."

As Kalar, unaware, wriggled into the open, Amarynth turned slowly, coming face to face with Prince Ka-Raamon.

CHAPTER 16

"Kalar," said Amarynth quietly, and something in her face as he looked up must have told him who was behind him, for he rolled to his feet and drew his sword in one fluid motion, only to find the prince's own silver blade at his throat.

"Kalar, is it?" the prince said easily. "Just put that kribiksticker away, won't you?"

Stiffly, the mountain youth complied. "So call your men," he growled.

"My men?" Ka-Raamon lowered his sword but did not sheathe it. "Oddly enough, I seem to have misplaced them."

"How did you find us?" Amarynth demanded.

"There are times my dear father shows a distressing tendency to rely on brute force to the exclusion of subtler methods," Ka-Raamon replied. "When he found where Herkas was hiding, he sent troops to storm the two entrances of which he was already aware. I, on the other hand, went to the library, found the records of the last time this place was attacked, many years ago when the City Elders still ruled and found it expedient to crack down on smuggling, and read there of this little bolt hole." He smiled. "And here I am."

"Why alone?" demanded Kalar. "To claim all the glory of capturing us?"

"Not at all," said the prince, and now he did sheathe his sword. "I've come to help you escape."

Kalar laughed, but Amarynth's heart beat faster. *More role-playing?* she wondered. *Or...* "Why?"

Her tone brought Kalar's head around. "Amarynth, he's lying! You don't believe—"

"He's here," she pointed out. "He's alone. And, whatever his reasons, he was kind to me. The least we can do is hear him out."

"But—" Kalar began, only to be smoothly cut off by the prince.

"Thank you," he said. "I shall be brief; escape is not something one should procrastinate about."

He smiled, but Amarynth was not yet ready to smile back. Twice before she had trusted Ramon; once he had led her to his father and once to the temple. This time, she would be more cautious.

The prince's smile didn't waver, despite her lack of response. "I was so angry at the way Elsdar had treated you that I sought him out last night—and found him with other Wanderers, at the temple."

Amarynth frowned. Surely he wasn't still trying to pretend Elsdar had acted alone…

But the prince wasn't finished. "And I found my father's messenger there as well, paying Elsdar well for bringing you here, with not a word said about the manner in which it was done, or about the abuses my father told you would be punished.

"I am not a fool. I did nothing to betray what I felt, and this morning I delivered you as promised to the temple, intending to face Thesman himself and learn the truth. I sensed you felt I had changed in some manner from last night; well, true enough." He shook his head ruefully. "But I never got to talk to Thesman. After I left you in his office, intending to wait in the corridor, I was removed rather forcibly by two very large Black Guards and a Wanderer, who told me it was my father's command I not be permitted to remain in the temple."

He looked full into Amarynth's eyes, and she saw only honesty in his face. "Of course my father knew what I discovered last night and must have known I would take exception to it. I charged back to the palace to face him but was told he was not seeing anyone. I waited, growing angrier, and was about to burst in on him uninvited when a messenger arrived with the news you had withdrawn from the Power before becoming a Wanderer and had been 'abducted' on the way back from the temple by armed men who slew two Black Guards." He shook his head. "Of course he knew where you were; did Herkas really think his lair secret? My father had been biding his time, infiltrating Herkas's force with spies and traitors, weakening it. In time he could have destroyed it easily. But your escape forced his hand. So he came roaring out of his tower, brushing past me as if I weren't there, calling for soldiers and weapons. And I—I went to the library, and then I came here."

"I don't believe a word of it," Kalar growled.

"Do *you*?" Ramon asked Amarynth softly.

"I was almost taken by the Beast, Ramon, because I trusted you and your father," she said. "Why should I trust you now?"

"Because I'm telling the truth."

Kalar snorted, and Amarynth shook her head. "That's not enough—" she began.

The prince cut her off. "Hide!" he commanded, and dashed away.

Amarynth stared after him, astonished, then suddenly registered approaching hoofbeats. Alongside Kalar, she flung herself to the ground behind the false bush that hid the tunnel.

The hoofbeats slowed, stopped. "Prince Ka-Raamon!" cried a breathless voice. "What are you—"

"There's another exit to that thieves' warren," the prince shouted.

Kalar groped for his sword, but Amarynth stopped his hand. "Listen!" she hissed.

"I came out to check it. The Spirit Singer girl and a boy jumped me and stole my therra."

"Are you all right?"

"A little bruised flesh, a little bruised pride." Amarynth could almost see his wry smile as he said it.

"How long ago?"

"Ten, maybe fifteen minutes. They set off north, circling the city!"

"Shall I leave an escort?"

"I can walk. But I have a score to settle. You just make sure you bring them back!"

"On a knaxen tether!" shouted someone, and then the therras galloped away.

Prince Ka-Raamon returned to the glade. Hands on his hips, he grinned down at Amarynth and Kalar. "Now," he said. "Just where do you want to escape to?"

Amarynth scrambled up. Kalar climbed to his feet more slowly, his eyes on Ka-Raamon, suspicion still plain on his face. Her own doubts were far from vanquished, but there was no denying they needed help. If this was just another role the prince was playing, that of naive lordling whose eyes had suddenly been opened, it might at least serve to get them away from the Havenheart. There was no need to tell him about the message from the far-off Singer or their final destination, not yet. Not until they were sure. "South," she said.

"Amarynth—" Kalar warned, but she ignored him.

"South?" The prince's left eyebrow arched. "The Haunted Mountains?"

"It won't be a pleasant journey," said Amarynth. "You need not share it. If you can just help us safely around the city..."

"Between ghosts and my father's wrath, I'll take ghosts." Amarynth couldn't help smiling at that, and Ramon grinned. "I'll wear down your defences yet!"

She wiped the smile away. "It's *your* defences, or at least your city's, we have to concern ourselves with now."

"We'll have to wait until nightfall," Kalar warned. "Every pair of eyes on the wall and road will be watching for us."

"We can't stay here, either," said the prince. "My deception will not last long; eventually they'll come seeking me. But Kalar is right about travelling by daylight. We must find a place to hide until dark."

Kalar looked slightly surprised to find Ka-Raamon agreeing with him but kept his combative tone. "And I suppose you know just the place."

"Indeed I do." The prince smiled at Amarynth and offered his arm. "My lady?"

Despite Kalar's glower, she took Ramon's arm, and let the prince lead her deeper into the woods.

He talked as they walked, just as if he were showing her the sights of Havenheart, as he had promised to do. "It's really very bad military form to have a forest this size nestled right up against the walls," he said as they picked their way through the undergrowth. He carefully avoided a patch of soft ground and lifted a branch out of the way instead of snapping it. Amarynth, glancing back, thought Kalar's glare softened a little at that evidence of care. "However," the prince continued, "it's only since my father became Master of the City that Havenheart has had walls. We were only fortunate no enemy came against us."

What enemy? Amarynth wondered: then, remembering her realization that the Beast fed on violence, felt cold. No doubt it would create one when it got hungry enough.

"Anyway," Ramon went on, "my father was going to have this wood cut down, but what with one thing and another he never got around to it. For which I was always grateful; he never knew it, but many times when he could not find me when he wanted me, and sent men all over the city seeking me, I wasn't even within the walls, but here." He leaped over a narrow brook and helped Amarynth across with the grace of a courtier from the old tales. Leaving Kalar to fend for himself, he continued. "I even built myself a rude shelter, just a lean-to really, but enough that I could come here even when it rained or snowed and have the comfort of walls and a roof of sorts, and even a fire—though," he added ruefully, "I would recommend against the latter this day."

Amarynth smiled again, and this time the expression stayed.

A little farther brought them to the shelter, just as rude as the prince had described, deplorably run down and, he confessed, much smaller than he remembered it. But it was well-hidden by a screen of bushes, the ground under its sloping roof was dry, and there was room for the three of them to hide there, able to see out without being seen.

Which they did, the prince falling silent rather abruptly, while Kalar sat blackly frowning and Amarynth leaned against one of the posts supporting the roof and slowly felt weariness fill her. The last thing she felt, before sleeping, was the prince's arm going around her shoulders, so that her head nestled not against rough wood but the smooth fabric covering his chest.

A gentle touch woke her some hours later. She found she was lying on the ground, the prince's cloak spread over her. The prince himself knelt by her head, smiling, his teeth white in the moonlight that had replaced the afternoon sunshine. "The ghosts await us in the mountains," he said. "There has been no alarm, but I'll feel better with a night's distance between us and my father."

"I'd feel better with a night's distance between us and you," Kalar said as he came back into the shelter. "No one's been back to the tunnel entrance since we left," he told Amarynth. "Suspicious."

Kalar's antipathy toward Spirit Singers seemed to have expanded to include the prince, and Amarynth was beginning to find it grating. "The most suspicious thing around here is you," she retorted. She got to her feet and stretched, reaching her arms up to touch the low roof, then dropping them to her sides again. "I can't say I'm looking forward to it, but...let's be going."

"I know the safest path around the city," said the prince. "Follow me."

"Follow him to the grave," Kalar muttered, but fell silent at a hard look from Amarynth.

It took them an hour, creeping from forest to hedgerow to stone to copse, to circle Havenheart's wall, always aware of the guards atop it, seeing the glint of their armour and hearing distant voices. But at last they were on the south side of the city and could see the saw-toothed outline of the Haunted Mountains against the stars, their black edges silvered with moonlit snow.

"A long, hard journey," said the prince.

"It won't be the first I've made," Amarynth said. "This time, at least, it's my choice and not your father's."

The prince said nothing.

"Can you say the same, Ka-Raamon?" Kalar demanded.

"Kalar!" Amarynth snapped. "Ramon has led us safely this far. Don't taunt him."

"It's all right." The prince glanced back at the city. "My father's reach is very long. Kalar is right to fear him."

"Fear him?" Kalar's hand went to his dagger. "You—"

"Quiet!" Amarynth glared at them both. "Fight at the journey's end, if you must; not its beginning. We have a long way to go."

"We do indeed," said Ramon, as Kalar subsided. The prince turned his face from Havenheart to the Haunted Mountains; and as they set out, he led the way.

For three days they crossed farmland, travelling always by night, and even so, keeping to windrows and the patches of forest that dotted even this long-civilized land. Gradually, the mountains took shape before them, until they were no longer distant shadows but hard-edged, snow-capped piles of rock, clad in dark forest, higher and more jagged than the Northern Range, which Amarynth had crossed and which was Kalar's birthplace. Here, Amarynth knew, she would find no villages nestled among the valleys. If legend were true, this was the abode of ghosts—and as a Spirit Singer, she knew better than to discount legends of ghosts out of hand.

Through all those three days there was no sign of pursuit, a fact Amarynth welcomed with thankfulness, not only for their own safety but because it seemed strong evidence the prince was, in fact, an ally and not a spy. But

Kalar greeted even their good fortune with suspicion. "Why should Ar-Naathon come after us?" he said privately one day to Amarynth. "His son marches with us."

"And has done nothing but help us since we started," Amarynth pointed out. "Kalar, I doubted him as much as you did at the beginning—but I'm beginning to think he has told us the truth."

"If we wait until he plays us false it will be too late!" Kalar retorted. "We should leave him behind, now, before we get any closer to our goal. He's lied to you twice, Amarynth—why trust him now?"

"We can use another ally," she said. "And if he truly has become one—as it appears he has, despite your suspicion—then he has given up more than any of us to see this hopeless task through, without even knowing what it is. How can we turn our back on an offer like that?"

"You're too trusting!"

"And you don't trust anyone."

"I trust myself."

"What kind of life is that?"

"A long one," said Kalar, and left her.

On the fourth day they began their journey in daylight, having passed the last farm the night before. The land changed, from gently rolling prairie to foothills, each successive ridge a little higher than the last; and that evening, as they climbed the tallest yet, Amarynth looked back across the hills to the plain—and saw fires.

Silently, she took Ramon's arm and pointed them out to him.

He showed no surprise. "So. I wondered how long it would take my father to realize we were not in Havenheart."

Despite her words to Kalar, Amarynth asked the question the mountain youth had raised. "Why so long? He told me himself he could sense me. If that's true, and he waited so long to come after us—it's almost as if he wanted us to escape."

"He can sense you, but not everywhere, and not always," said the prince. "He has to concentrate on a particular area for a time, and if he does not detect your presence, move on. As long as you are in the Lower World, that is; he says he can sense Singers almost instantly when they enter the Between World."

"Because of the Beast," muttered Amarynth.

"Exactly." Ramon kept looking at those distant camp-fires. "Only Black Guards will be in that party: a dozen at least, maybe more."

Amarynth turned away. "We'll just have to reach our destination before they can catch us." She descended to the clearing on the far side of the ridge where Kalar was building their own fire, well-hidden by an outcropping of rock. Ramon followed her.

"Just what *is* our destination?" he said. "You've never told me anything beyond the fact it lies in the Haunted Mountains."

"And that was too much," said Kalar.

The prince sighed and sat on a rock near the fire. "How can I prove my trustworthiness? Whenever I help you, you say it's for my own ends."

"Go back and lead away the men following us," Kalar shot back. "Leave us. Then we'll know you aren't just using us."

"You'll need my sword should they find you," the prince pointed out. "And what makes you think I *could* lead those men away from your trail? No doubt my father wants me, but he wants you more."

"A well-reasoned excuse."

"Stop it!" Amarynth snapped. She turned to Ramon. "We do value your help—or at least, I do." She gave Kalar a hard glance, then lowered herself to the ground next to the prince and reached for her pack. "If it's any consolation, Kalar doesn't trust me, either. Or any Spirit Singer. Or any living person, for that matter."

"If you really value my aid, how come *you* won't answer my questions?" Ramon asked.

For a moment, Amarynth said nothing. She rummaged in her pack for a loaf of bread, poked a chunk of it on the end of a long stick, and held it in the fire to toast. After staring into the flames a moment, she finally made up her mind. "I'll tell you this much," she said. "We're going to meet someone, someone who thinks he can help us."

"But how did you find out about this 'someone'?" Prince Ramon held out his hands to the warmth. "Did he send a message?"

"In a manner of speaking." Amarynth pulled the hot bread from the stick and bounced it from hand to hand to cool it enough to eat. "He's looking for me, or someone like me. I don't know why."

"It sounds to me like you're trusting this mysterious stranger with rather a lot—like your life." The prince smiled crookedly. "Odd you won't even trust me with the truth."

"That *is* the truth," said Amarynth.

"Not all of it, I think," Ramon replied. "But no matter. At least it explains why my father is so anxious to get you back. Perhaps he intercepted this mysterious message you won't tell me about, or one of his spies learned of it. He knows you are vital to those opposing him."

Kalar grunted, but said nothing; Amarynth, likewise silent, bit into her toasted bread, thinking of Ar-Naathon's power—or rather, the power he had gained by Linking with the monster in the Between World. He could sense where she was even now; had always been able to, even when she dwelt in her grandfather's tower. He could look into the minds of those who were linked to him through the Beast. She shuddered at the thought of how close she had come to being subsumed by that black creature and herself becoming a Wanderer.

The prince kept talking. "How much farther is this mysterious destination? We must think about supplies. Water should be no problem, but food may be."

Amarynth swallowed her bread. "We have enough

for another day or two. But we didn't get out with all our supplies—our guide was killed." She said a quick prayer for his spirit, and hoped the Singers still lived to minister to all those who had died in the battle in the warren, less it became an abode of haunts as dread as the mountains they were about to enter.

"We'll have to hunt, then," said Ramon. "We'll need a bow."

"That," said Kalar, standing and brushing dirt from his hands, "is best left to me. As is the hunting."

"I *have* hunted," said the prince mildly.

"No doubt." Kalar's tone dripped scorn. "But we have no beaters or pikemen. This hunting will involve only one man and one animal, and I have survived by such skills since your Black Guards killed my father."

Ramon looked at him coldly. "Have it your way, then."

Kalar bent over and rummaged in his pack. "I have a bowstring—" he began; and then Amarynth screamed.

Out of the forest behind Kalar loomed the armoured figure of a Black Guard, a huge iron war-hammer clutched in one hand. Kalar reacted as quickly as a korg, ducking the first blow and throwing himself at the Guard's legs, bringing the man crashing to the ground in a thunderous rattle of steel. Kalar regained his feet first, but backed away, swearing; his sword lay beneath the Guard, who was just struggling up on one knee.

Ramon snatched his own sword from the ground, and it hissed from the scabbard as he leaped the fire. The

Guard's hammer stirred the wind but missed the prince, whose first stroke bounced off the black helmet.

The Guard shook his head as though annoyed by an insect, and regained his feet, looming over the prince, who stood at guard. Kalar drew his dagger and advanced, and Amarynth snatched a burning brand from the fire and circled behind the armoured man, whose head swung from side to side as he tried to watch them all. The prince lunged, but the Guard's hammer knocked his sword away, and Ramon, leaping backward, barely escaped a return stroke that would have smashed his skull.

Amarynth and Kalar dashed forward, Amarynth swinging her brand at the base of the Guard's helmet and Kalar striving to get his dagger in any chink in the harness, but the Guard's mailed left hand crashed into Amarynth's jaw with blinding force and sent her tumbling, and his broad right shoulder thudded into Kalar's chest and smashed him to the ground, gasping for breath, his dagger hopelessly out of reach.

As the clearing spun around her, Amarynth saw the Guard suddenly charge Ramon, hammer whirling, heard the crash of metal to metal, saw both Guard and prince go down—and then saw Ramon stand again, alone, blood staining the firelit edge of his sword and the front of his tunic.

He limped over to her, and she managed to haul herself to a sitting position, skull throbbing. The prince knelt beside her. "Are you all right?"

"Wonderful," she said with difficulty; her jaw was stiffening. She cautiously felt her teeth with her tongue; they all still seemed to be present, though she imagined one or two felt loose. "I'll just sit here a bit, if you don't mind."

"You were very brave," Ramon said seriously, touching the bruised place so tenderly it didn't even hurt; then he rose and went back to the fallen Guard.

Kalar was also struggling upright, holding his stomach and gasping, face greenish-white. The prince wiped his sword on the Guard's black cloak and sheathed the blade; then he rolled the dead man over, tugged free something he carried, and handed it to Kalar. "Yours," he said. "Good hunting. I'm going to see if there are any more Black Guards around." Then he strode out of the clearing.

Kalar looked down at the bow in his hand, and painfully began to laugh.

CHAPTER 18

For a time all Amarynth could think of was the pain in her head, but gradually it came to her that something was subtly wrong. Slowly she raised her eyes, wincing at the throbbing inside her skull, and looked around the clearing.

Kalar sat by the fire on the rock the prince had vacated to save his life, running his hand over the smooth dark wood of the Black Guard's bow. Her gaze travelled from him to the dead Guard, lying where he had fallen, black armour glinting dully in the firelight. The wrongness lay in that direction; she struggled to her feet, staggering a little as, for a moment, it felt as if her head would burst, then, a bit steadier, walked over to the corpse.

The Guard's sword-cut body was not a pleasant sight, but Amarynth had seen worse laid out upon the dais in her grandfather's Spirit Chamber. And with that thought she suddenly knew what was wrong. She blamed the fog of pain for blocking it from her before.

I can't sense his spirit!

The realization was so shocking she dropped to her knees, and suddenly Kalar was beside her, his hand under her arm, pulling her up. "Are you all right?"

"He has no spirit!" she whispered. "Or else—" Her voice closed on the words, but her mind completed them inexorably. *Or else I've lost my Gift.*

The former was impossible, the latter unthinkable. Her hands were tangled in her cloak; she raised a fold of the heavy material and bit it to keep from screaming.

"I don't understand," Kalar said.

"Don't understand what?" The prince had returned; his sword, clean and bright once more, whispered back into its sheath. "I've circled the camp; there are no more Black Guards. This one may have been sent out as a scout, but got his orders confused; they're not too bright..." His voice trailed off as, for the first time, he became aware of Amarynth's distress. He touched her bruised cheek gently. "Amarynth, what's wrong?"

Kalar stiffened and Amarynth felt his hand fall away as she reached out and clutched Ramon's fingers. "I can't sense him," she cried. "There should be something—no one has Sung him, his spirit has to be right here, tied to his body—but I can't—"

The prince pulled her to him, holding her tightly. "I was afraid this might have happened," he murmured.

She pushed away and wiped tears from her face. "What?"

Ramon's face was grave. "Sometimes—oh, Amarynth, I'm so sorry—sometimes those who face the Beast to become Wanderers don't become Wanderers—sometimes, they simply lose the Gift."

Amarynth's head throbbed harder. "But I ran. I never touched—"

"I know, I know. But you were close. No one has ever been as close as you were and run, my father said. Maybe..." He shook his head. "Maybe you got too close."

"No!" Amarynth turned away, but that only brought the fallen Guard back into her sight—the dead man who lay there, impossibly soulless. Suddenly she was sure it was true. "Then I'm a Spirit Singer no longer!" she whispered.

She thought she glimpsed an echo of her own anguish on Kalar's face, but when she raised her head to look directly at him his expression was stolid. "Welcome to the real world," he said, and turned back toward the fire and the Black Guard's bow.

Gently Ramon touched her shoulder and turned her to face him. "The Gift might return. Like you said, you aren't a Wanderer; you never actually touched the Beast..."

"If it's gone, and the Beast took it, how can it come back?" Amarynth cried. "Without it I can't even enter the Between World where the Beast is." Another thought shook her. "We're lost!" she gasped, eyes wide. "I'm no longer a Singer. The one who sent the message—I don't qualify anymore!"

Ramon stared at her. "You're not going to abandon—"

"Why not?" A strange sense of freedom gripped Amarynth. What if it were true? What if, at last, she was no longer Amarynth, apprentice Spirit Singer, but only Amarynth, young woman? Hadn't she often wished for this very thing? "Why not?" she cried again. "I can't do whatever it is he wants me to do—I never could. I'm useless to him. Why should I climb Icethorn Peak?"

Kalar turned toward her in shock and the prince's eyes widened. "Icethorn—"

Amarynth laughed. "Yes, Icethorn Peak. That's our destination, Ramon. That's our terrible secret. What difference does it make who knows it now? We'll lead Ar-Naathon on a wild goose chase. West to the coast, take a ship back to Covedrift—he'll never find the one who sent that message!"

The prince seized her shoulders, almost angrily, and shook her. "Amarynth, no!" She winced, and he released her at once. "I'm sorry. But you must listen to me. You're talking nonsense. You don't *know* that you're useless to this mysterious Messenger until he tells you. Whatever he is, he's very powerful. If your Gift is lost, he may be the only one who can get it back!"

"If he could face the Beast alone he already would have!" she cried.

"You don't know that. And Amarynth—if you

abandon this, if you go back to Covedrift—then what? They sent you out to find a Singer or become one. If you go back empty-handed—you know what that means to your village. It will die. Even if you can't Sing, you have to find someone who can. And no one can while the Beast is there. Except, just possibly—"

"The Messenger." The brief euphoria faded. Even if she were no longer a Singer, she still bore the responsibility of one. She looked at Kalar. *Like him and his "sacred duty." His father is dead, but the duty was passed on...Grandfather left me a duty, too. I accepted it, promised the village elders to find a Singer for Covedrift, even if I couldn't do it myself.*

She remembered the concern in the elders' faces as she set out; how could she disappoint them? Already there would be murmuring in the village, people wondering if they should leave...and if there had been another death...

The other possibility, that the Wanderers were there already, she did not want to consider.

"You can't let them down." Ramon's eyes burned into hers. "Or the ones in Havenheart who sent you out." He paused. "Or yourself."

Or Timara, Amarynth thought, but did not say. Ramon did not know about that poor babe, trapped in the Between World, bound to Amarynth so that only she could lead her to the Gate.

"All right," she said. "All right! We go on."

An odd expression flitted across Ramon's face, one almost of sadness; but then he summoned a grin and hugged her so tightly she winced again. "Gently, gently," she pleaded, her voice muffled by his shoulder. "My head feels like it's going to fall off."

Ramon let her go. "I'm so sorry, I forgot—lie down. Sleep. Kalar and I will keep watch."

Amarynth glanced at Kalar, who was counting arrows. "How could I be any safer?" With the prince's help, she retrieved her pack and spread her bedroll near the fire, which Ramon had built up again. Lying down, Amarynth found, greatly eased the pain in her head, and her new determination to press on helped relieve the small voice of terror whispering in the back of her mind that now she would never be a Singer, never, never...

She slept, plagued by bad dreams that vanished with the morning but left her with vague foreboding. Ramon woke her and she opened her eyes to see pink dawn-light tingeing the tops of the trees surrounding their clearing. "How do you feel?" the prince asked.

Cautiously, she sat up. Her head throbbed, but not as much as she had feared; the side of her face, however, was badly swollen, her jaw so stiff she could barely talk. "I can travel," she managed to croak.

"Good." The prince helped her to her feet, then rolled her bedroll and stuffed it back in her pack. "Kalar has gone ahead, hunting."

"He trusts—" The sentence Amarynth intended was too long to complete, but the prince understood.

"Kalar has decided, since I saved his life last night, that perhaps I am not quite the villain he thought. He no longer fears I will kill you or abduct you the moment his back is turned." Ramon looked around at the dark forest. "Unless, of course, he's watching me right now with an arrow nocked."

Amarynth chuckled—and immediately wished she hadn't.

They travelled deeper into the mountains through the day and saw neither Kalar nor any pursuers. Though Amarynth could not talk comfortably, the prince could and did, about nothing in particular. Trees and flowers and birds were worthy of comment; of his own life he said little, except for rare and passing references to people and places in the city. Not once did he mention his father, or Wanderers, or Spirit Singers, or the Beast; it was almost as if he wanted to forget they existed. Amarynth had no quarrel with that, for she felt the same way.

Sunshine accompanied them as they climbed through green meadows and waded tossing seas of purple flowers, insects buzzing around them. Amarynth let the simple joys of good weather, good companionship—a rarity in her life—and fresh air absorb her, and was almost sorry, as the sun descended, to see Kalar waiting for them at the top of the next ridge, carrying a pair of long-eared rock finxes.

Roasted over a small, well-hidden fire, the creatures made him and Ramon a fine meal. Amarynth had to content herself with broth and a few slivers of meat small enough to swallow without chewing. Ramon fed them to her, and she looked into his laughing eyes and wondered how she could ever have mistrusted him. *No more roles*, she thought. *Today I saw the true Ka-Raamon.*

Or just the one you most wish *was the true one?* a small voice asked deep in her mind, but she ignored it.

The prince winked at her, and she laughed. That hurt, so she tried to scowl at him, but that only made her laugh more; and despite the pain and the reasons for it, she realized she was happy.

And then she looked past Ramon and saw the black, featureless shape of someone standing in the shadows.

She stiffened. "Black Guard!" she whispered, and a look of almost comical astonishment crossed the prince's face before he turned to see.

Kalar rose and drew his sword, but the prince leaped up and grabbed his arm. "Your sword will do you no good!"

"You killed one last night," growled Kalar. "What you did, I can do."

"I killed a Black Guard," said Ramon. "A creature of flesh. There's no flesh about *that*."

Amarynth rose to her feet. "A ghost?"

"Stay here," said the prince. Slowly he crossed toward the shadowy figure, and as he did, Amarynth became aware of more indistinct shapes among the trees, all around them, solidifying into naked human form, until it seemed they were surrounded by a huge, unnaturally silent crowd. Pale eyes glittered like the ice on the peaks, and a cold, cold breath seeped across the ground, slowly rising, an inexorable tide, a breath from the empty expanses of the Between World.

Amarynth could hardly breathe. *Ghosts have no power but fear*, she told herself. *Ghosts have no power but fear*...but fear was quite enough. And there were so many of them! How could there be so many unSung dead in a place where no one had ever lived, from the First Landing to this day?

The prince had reached the first apparition. "You know who I am?" he said sternly.

Voices like the hiss of wind-blown snow scouring a frozen lake answered from all around, "We do."

"Then why do you trouble me and my companions?"

Laughter, eerie and cold, sent a shiver through Amarynth. "We march with you, Prince Ka-Raamon. To your journey's end...and beyond."

"We have no need of your company."

"You have no choice." Again that icy mirth swirled around them. "But you will not see us again...until the end."

The immaterial multitude vanished, and the rising wave of freezing air ebbed from around Amarynth's feet.

The prince turned, looking troubled. Kalar's face was pale, even in the ruddy glow of the firelight. "I do not believe in ghosts," he said slowly, each word emphasized.

"Then what did you just see?" the prince snapped at him. "Do you mistrust your own eyes, too?"

Kalar's head whipped around and his fingers tightened on the sword, which he had never sheathed. But the prince turned his back on him and returned to the fire, staring into it, not meeting Amarynth's eyes.

"Why did you ask if they knew you?" she mumbled through her still stiff and aching jaw.

"They dwell in the Between World," he said, almost in a mutter. "They must fear the Power...they must! And they must know my——" He stopped suddenly, then looked up and spoke in a much clearer voice. "They must know my father," he said. "I hoped they did not also know of the rift between us. I hoped their fear of him might make them leave us alone."

"They did." *But they didn't sound afraid*, Amarynth thought.

"Yes." The prince still looked unhappy.

All three of them sat up that night around the fire rather later than they normally would have, but the ghosts did not return, and if occasionally there was a distant sound like hissing laughter, it could just as easily have been the wind in the trees.

Amarynth hoped Kalar would hunt again the next day and leave her with Ramon. His startling transformation upon facing the spirits had troubled her, and she hoped to be able to question him. The pain in her jaw had receded, and she thought she could talk almost normally again. But instead, it was the Guesthost's son who woke her. "The prince hunts," he said shortly. "Let's move."

Amarynth was once more able to chew and talk, but Kalar showed no interest in conversation, either during her brief, hurried breakfast, or as they continued their mostly uphill journey. He walked several steps ahead of her, one hand on his sword hilt, his eyes constantly scanning the forest. Amarynth toiled steadily after him, occasionally giving him a glare that should have scorched his cloak, but he seemed unaware.

Crossing one high, rocky pasture, she tripped over a hidden stone and fell, gasping. Almost instantly, Kalar was there to help her to her feet, but when he saw she was all right the concerned look she had almost convinced herself she had seen on his face gave way to stolid indifference.

That night Ramon met them with a tiny mountain burla, and with its meat stored in their backpacks, they travelled the next two days together. As night followed night without another appearance of their ghostly companions, Amarynth quit jumping at every shadow cast by the firelight and every crack of cooling rock, but she could not cast off the sense of foreboding the spirit's words had given her. *You will not see us again...until the end.*

The end of what? she wondered. She had no answer; but it had a finality to it she did not like.

The cheerful, child-like Ramon she had known during their one day alone together seemed to have vanished with the spirits. Most of the time he didn't talk at all; once, when Amarynth came up behind him without his being aware of it and touched him on the shoulder, he whirled around so fast he came within an inch of striking her across the face, and then he didn't really apologize, but only muttered, "Sorry," and turned away again.

The tension between Ramon and Kalar became almost palpable whenever they were close to each other, as though only immense restraint kept them from coming to blows. Since the prince wouldn't talk, after the first day of their travelling together once more, Amarynth approached Kalar alone.

He sat with his back to a tree at the verge of the firelight, sharpening his dagger on a whetstone he carried in his belt pouch. The rhythmic hiss of stone on steel faltered for an instant as Amarynth approached.

She sat down beside him and gazed at the fire, where Ramon, apparently indifferent to them, sat staring into the flames. "I thought things were getting better between you two," she said finally. "But ever since the spirits—"

"When he killed the Black Guard I thought we might be able to trust him," Kalar said gruffly. "Not anymore."

"What's changed?" Amarynth pulled a tuft of grass from the ground and slowly shredded it, blade by blade.

"You can't tell me you haven't noticed!"

Amarynth sighed. "Of course I have. But I was wondering if we see the same thing."

Kalar quit sharpening and held the dagger up so that its blade caught the firelight, then glanced along its shining length at the prince. "I don't think we've ever seen the true Ka-Raamon," he said bluntly. "He's like a scaly little twisk, always changing colour to match the background. Maybe the way he's been the last two days is the real prince. Maybe it isn't. Maybe he's still got another face to show us. Whatever, I don't trust someone who changes so much."

"Maybe he's got a good reason."

"Such as?"

"Maybe he's scared."

Kalar snorted.

Amarynth gave him a hard look. "Aren't you?"

"Nothing has frightened me since I saw my father die, because nothing could be worse than that." He stood and looked down at her. "You're still trying to make excuses for him. You still want to trust him. Well, I tried it for a while, and it didn't work." He drove his knife back into its sheath. "But then, I'm not falling in love with him!"

Amarynth gaped at him as he strode away. *Falling in —nonsense!* she thought fiercely, though her face was burning. *Of course I want to trust the prince! However strange he behaves, he saved my life and Kalar's and got us safely away from Havenheart. Hasn't he earned a little trust? Love has nothing to do with it.*

Angrily she scrambled to her feet and returned to the fire, squatting beside it and stirring its hot heart with a stick. She glanced sidelong at the prince. The leaping flames made his golden hair sparkle, but cast deep shadows on his lean face, bringing out his cheekbones and brows. She searched for some sign of duplicity or evil but could see nothing but grimness.

Ramon didn't seem to notice her scrutiny; but a long time after she had rolled herself in her bedroll and slept, she half-woke and saw him looking at her with terrible sadness and longing. Yet in the morning, his face was as closed as ever. *A dream*, she told herself.

The mountains seemed to grow as they climbed among them, while the plains behind them shrank into insignificance, until it seemed the whole world must be made of soaring black peaks and the vast heartland of Haven was only a tiny valley.

Finally they reached the top of a high pass and looked beyond to a peak standing apart from its neighbours and above them all, razor-sharp slopes encased in ice.

"Icethorn," said Ramon dully. "Another day, two at most, and we'll have found your Messenger."

"If the Black Guards don't find us first," she said.

"They won't."

Kalar gave him a pointed look. "How do you know?"

Ramon blinked and suddenly grinned. It reminded Amarynth of the sun emerging from behind a thundercloud. "Why, friend Kalar, I don't—but I have hopes. Armoured men cannot climb as fast as we can. We have gained on them, I think, since we saw their fires behind us; I would say we will have a lead of at least one day, and maybe two, when we reach Icethorn." His grin widened. "Do you still mistrust me?"

Kalar turned away without speaking. Ramon shrugged and actually gave Amarynth a wink. "Almost there," he said gaily. "I admit I looking forward to this. I haven't gone mountain-climbing in years." He set out after Kalar, leaving Amarynth to bring up the rear, staring at the back of his blonde head.

The Ramon from before the appearance of the spirits had returned, between one breath and the next. Although she had missed that version of him, Amarynth wasn't at all sure she trusted its abrupt reappearance.

She raised her eyes from the prince to Icethorn, waiting for them; and though their descent into the lowland surrounding the peak was gentle, Amarynth felt almost as though she were sliding helplessly down one of the mountain's ice-clad slopes, falling into the unknown.

They camped high in the pass that night, but by noon the next day were crossing the plain surrounding Icethorn, a barren, inhospitable place of thorny scrub, iron-grey brush, and hard black rock, broken by an occasional patch of yellowing grass. A palpable chill flowed from the frozen heights of the mountain, a disquieting reminder of the unearthly cold that had accompanied the spirit host, a breath of the alien air of the Between World.

Yet nothing seemed to affect Ramon's abruptly regained cheerfulness. At one point he even broke into a chorus of the drinking song he had whistled the night he escorted Amarynth to Ar-Naathon, this time with no sign of embarrassment at all, though the lyrics were just as bawdy as Amarynth had imagined them.

Kalar, even more silent than usual, lagged behind the other two, to better keep an eye on Ramon, Amarynth supposed. She was almost glad of it; Ramon's gaiety when there was no cause for it troubled her far more than his surly silence following the visit by the spirit host.

As the land rose toward the sere lower slopes of Icethorn, Amarynth began looking for the marks the Havenheart Singers had told her would be there; and finally, just as the sun touched the mountains to the west, she saw the first, a pale slash on a dark rock, exactly like the marks that had led her up the Crag the night Kalar rescued her. She pointed them out to Ramon. "We've made it," she cried. "All we have to do is follow those up the mountain, and we'll find the Messenger."

The grin that had been almost constantly on the prince's face that day suddenly faded. He looked at the mark, then at the sky. "Let's camp here," he said in a low voice. "Otherwise we'll be climbing in the dark."

Amarynth started to protest; then decided Ramon was right. Calling to Kalar, she shrugged out of the straps of her pack and began gathering wood for a fire.

Kalar joined them crossly. "The marks are clear; we needn't stop."

"They may not be so clear further on," said Ramon. "And as the way grows steeper there will be fewer places to camp. I wouldn't want to spend the night crouched on a cliff ledge waiting for dawn."

"Hmmmph." Kalar unshipped his bow and quiver and set them by Amarynth's growing pile of wood. "If Black Guards are in the pass they'll see a fire," he noted pointedly, and Amarynth hesitated.

"The Black Guards will not come tonight," the prince said, and when Amarynth glanced up at him, startled by the certainty in his tone, he added simply, "I know their ways." He turned and looked back down their trail, and Amarynth, pressing her lips together, turned to the task of lighting the recalcitrant brushwood.

The tinder finally caught, and then the wood ignited, giving off flaring yellow light and oily black smoke that wove a pillar through the still air high up to where the sun still shone. "Another marker for the Black Guards to follow," muttered Kalar. But he roasted the last of the leaf-wrapped burla meat from his pack just the same.

When they had eaten, and night had fully descended, the prince stood and held out his hand to Amarynth. "Walk with me," he said, his face hooded in fire-cast shadow, and she stood and followed him into the darkness, while Kalar stared suspiciously after them.

Ramon led her back along their trail until the fire became a tiny spark of light at the base of the huge black monolith of Icethorn. The prince looked up to where stars glinted faintly off the mountain's snows, then said abruptly, his hold on Amarynth's hand tightening, "Don't go up there."

It was like a jolt of cold water in her face. She pulled free. "*What?*"

He didn't look at her, keeping his eyes on the peak. "I know I said differently just a few days ago. I was wrong. I shouldn't have told you to keep on with this quest. It's too dangerous. You should leave. You should go home."

"Go home?" Amarynth glared at his shadowy form. "Go *home?* Go home to what? As you reminded me, my people sent me to find a Spirit Singer or become one! I can't go home until I've done one or the other."

"So go find a Spirit Singer!" The prince turned toward her then, his voice rising. "The Wanderers haven't reached all of Haven. There are still true Singers out there. Find one. Take him home with you. But don't go up this mountain!"

Amarynth shook her head, bewildered. "What's come over you? Nothing's changed from when I made up my mind—when you *helped* me make up my mind—to finish my quest." She paused. "Or has it?"

"I hadn't thought it through, that's all. I hadn't—I didn't appreciate the danger. Don't you see, Amarynth?" His tone turned pleading. "You're going to get caught in the middle of a war—maybe a war in two worlds! If this Messenger has any followers there'll be fighting when the Black Guards get here, and whether he has any followers or not you know there'll be a battle in the Between World. You'll be in danger, body and soul—all for the sake of four old men in the city. It's not worth it, Amarynth. Leave, while you still can!"

"Do you really think running would put me out of danger? If I made it out of the mountains, where in Haven could I go that your father couldn't find me? As for the Between World—" She laughed bitterly. "I can't even enter the Between World, remember? My Gift is gone!"

"Then do it for me! You care for me, don't you?"

"Yes!" Amarynth surprised herself with the force of feeling behind the word. "But——"

"Well, I care for you, too!" Ramon paused. "Deeply," he said in a voice grown suddenly soft. "More deeply than I realized until tonight. More deeply than I've ever cared about anyone. You're the first girl who hasn't liked me just because I'm the prince, who has just treated me like an ordinary person..." Amarynth, hearing the echo of her own thoughts in his words, could not speak. He took her hands again. "I don't want to see you hurt, Amarynth. You've come this far—leave it, now, while you still can."

"But don't you see?" Amarynth said after a moment, when she could find her voice. "It's *because* I have come this far that I can't quit now. We're on the very edge of Icethorn, Ramon. We're almost there. You helped me get here. If I quit now I'd be saying everything we've gone through has been for nothing!" She squeezed his fingers. "And I have a duty. As a prince, you must understand duty."

"But——" Abruptly the prince's voice choked off, and he straightened and stiffened. When he spoke again his voice was almost cold. "Yes," he said. "I know duty."

"Then you understand?"

"Perfectly." He took a deep breath. "I'm going for a walk." And with that he spun and strode away.

Amarynth stared after him for a long time, even after he had vanished into the darkness, hearing his footsteps on the rocks dwindling into the distance, a fearful seed of uncertainty sprouting in her heart.

She made her way slowly back to the fire. Kalar looked up at her, his expression unreadable. "Where's the prince?"

"Gone for a walk." She held out chilled hands to the flames. "He'll be back," she said with all the certainty she could muster.

"He will not," said a clear voice from the darkness, and Amarynth and Kalar both jerked to their feet, Kalar's sword hissing from its sheath.

"What do you want, spirit?" he cried, his voice unnaturally high.

A smaller bit of blackness detached itself from the silhouette of the mountain, taking form and shape as it moved into the dim light of the fire, becoming at last an old man, bent and brown, leaning on a knobby staff. He wore a bedraggled white robe with a hood, and around his neck...

Amarynth gasped. Around his neck hung an Emblem, dark at first, that suddenly blazed the deepest purple she had ever seen.

Kalar stepped between her and the strange Spirit Singer. "No farther," he ordered harshly. "Ghosts have no power over the living but fear. You cannot harm us."

"Kalar—" Amarynth began, but the old man only raised one bushy white eyebrow.

"One shouldn't make such a sweeping statement without more knowledge about the matter, my boy," he said. "But in any event, I have no wish to harm you—even though you are trespassing on my mountain."

"Your—" Amarynth moved up beside Kalar, who never took his eyes off the old man. "You're the Messenger!"

The old man laughed, such a joyful sound that Amarynth found herself grinning at him and even Kalar looked hard-pressed to suppress a smile, though he also managed to look outraged at his own reaction. "Is that what you've taken to calling me? And as a formal title, yet—I can hear it in your voice. 'The Messenger.'" He said it in such a droll, deep-voiced way that even Kalar could control himself no longer and chuckled, lowering his blade.

The old man bowed low. "Indeed, yes, young lady, I am 'The Messenger.' At least, I am the one who sent the message to the Singers of the City. And you, as I know full well, are the one I asked them to send me."

"Yes, I'm—"

"Amarynth," said the Messenger. "Granddaughter of Nikos, Spirit Singer of Covedrift for half a century."

Amarynth gaped. "How do you—"

"Oh, I knew your grandfather well." The Messenger cocked an eye at Kalar. "And your friend here with the blade is Kalar, son of Arval, Guesthost of Snowdeep."

Kalar's expression went cold again. "You know too much."

The Messenger smiled sadly. "Yes," he said. "I do."

Amarynth looked over her shoulder, then back at the

old man. "Why do you say Ramon won't be back? Has something happened to him?"

"For some time I hoped it would—but alas, it wasn't to be. No, my child, nothing has happened to him. He is once more about the task his father set him. He has found the way to my lair, and now he hurries back to the Black Guards who are only hours behind you."

Amarynth stiffened. "You're lying!" she shouted, as though saying it loudly enough would make it true. "He wouldn't betray us—not after so long. He saved our lives —both our lives! He guided us away from the city—"

The Messenger sighed. "Ka-Raamon is his father's son, in more ways than one, my child. He is the most powerful Wanderer of them all, bound so closely to Ar-Naathon that his father can use him almost as an extension of himself. He has rarely been free of his father's influence, if not his actual presence, since you left Havenheart."

"No!" Amarynth felt hot tears on her cheeks, though whether of sorrow or fury she couldn't have said. "No, I won't believe it! He—he loves me!"

Kalar turned an angry glare on her, but the Messenger forestalled whatever he might have said. "As nearly as he loves anyone, yes, he does," he said quietly. "I was quite astonished; several times during your journey Ka-Raamon fought free of his father's influence, if only for a few moments, because of his growing love for you. And tonight—I would not have believed it if I had not witnessed it. He actually went against his father's will long enough to try to convince you to flee. He was trying to save your life. I almost thought he would break free entirely. But in the end—" The Messenger shook his head. "Ar-Naathon was too powerful, and Ka-Raamon too well-trained to obedience and the glory of his own power."

"No," Amarynth whispered.

Kalar suddenly brought his sword up again. "So the prince has betrayed us," he snarled. "Why should we give you the same opportunity?"

"Let be, boy," said the Messenger. "This quest is not yours. It is Amarynth's. Protect her, by all means; but you must let her decide what to do." He moved past Kalar and gently wiped the tears from Amarynth's cheeks with one gnarled finger. "Wait here for the prince to return and you will still be waiting when the Black Guards arrive. Flee as the prince urged you, and sooner or later, Black Guards or Wanderers will find you, and you will not escape again. Or come with me, now, to my cave; and let me show you how to defeat them."

Amarynth jerked away from him. "Defeat them?" she cried. "How?" She reached inside her blouse and pulled out her dark Emblem. "I'm no Spirit Singer! I'm not even an apprentice! My Gift is gone! You're so all-knowing, how come you didn't know that?"

Concern filled the Messenger's eyes and he reached out quickly to touch her forehead, his face intent. But then his expression lightened, and he withdrew his hand.

"My child," he said, "That is another of Ar-Naathon's lies."

"But when the Black Guard died I sensed no spirit!"

"Because there was none to sense. The Black Guards' spirits have been swallowed by the Beast—fed to it by the one you call Ar-Naathon. They are mindless creatures, dead already, their bodies moving only to the command of the Beast, through the Wanderers."

Amarynth swayed. *Too many shocks*, she thought dimly. "I need to think."

"My cave," said the Messenger, "is admirably suited to that purpose." Amarynth nodded, and he turned and led the way up the mountain, Kalar following sullenly.

Behind them the fire flickered twice, then went out.

CHAPTER 20

Amarynth had a moment to wonder how they could climb Icethorn in the dark, then realized that ahead of them the path glowed with its own moon-white light, winding up and up among the crags. Behind them the glow faded within a few feet. "No Spirit Singer can do that," Kalar whispered to her, nodding at the lighted path. "He's not what he says he is."

"You said you don't believe 'Death Squawkers' can do anything." Amarynth glanced black. "Anyway, would you like to try escaping down Icethorn blind?"

Kalar muttered something she didn't catch and fell back a pace.

The way took them through deep clefts in the mountain's side, up shale-strewn slopes, and through pockets of tangled brush, zigzagging back and forth until Amarynth doubted they could have found the path alone, even in daylight and with the marks to help. Loose rock shifted frighteningly beneath their feet and thorns caught at their clothing, and in places the path was so steep they had to use feet and hands together. Before an hour had gone they were climbing over crusted patches of snow and ice-covered stone, and weariness was settling into Amarynth's limbs like lead. But the old man never looked back, climbing tirelessly, not even breathing hard, always ten paces or so ahead of them.

Amarynth *was* breathing hard, almost gasping, and behind her she could hear Kalar, mountain-born though he was, gulping air and occasionally expelling it with a curse. *Just one more slope*, she told herself, *just one more slope*; but always there was one more beyond that, and then another, and she began to wonder, almost deliriously, if the Messenger really were a vengeful spirit leading them to destruction.

Wearily she took another step, calf burning—and her foot found no rock. With a soundless gasp she started to fall into emptiness to the left of the trail, afforded a horrifying glimpse of ice-covered boulders gleaming far below before Kalar's strong hand seized her arm and pulled her back to safety.

She spun away from the cliff edge and clung to him, seizing fistfuls of his tunic, burying her head on his chest and shaking uncontrollably—as was he. He patted her awkwardly on the back. "It's all right," he said hoarsely. "Nothing happened." And then, in sudden anger, he shouted, "You hear that? Nothing happened! Your scheme didn't work!"

"Kalar—" Amarynth pulled herself upright and tried to stop trembling. "If he wanted to kill us he could have done it a dozen times. It was my fault. I wasn't watching where I was going." She swayed a little and Kalar quickly reached for her again. "I'm so tired," she whispered.

"I'm sorry." For the first time since they had left the fire, the Messenger joined them. "I should have thought —I promise you, we're almost there."

"She could have been killed," Kalar said accusingly. "She was already exhausted before we started climbing."

"Kalar—" Amarynth took a deep breath and said to the Messenger, "I can go on a little farther."

"That's all that is necessary," he assured her, and turned to lead the way once more.

The surge of fear had lifted some of her fatigue, Amarynth found as they resumed the climb, but she could feel it inside waiting for her, like the Beast waited in the Between World.

She shuddered, wondering anew how the Messenger could fight such a monster—and what he needed her for. "I can't face it again," she whispered to herself. "I'll help any way I can—except that."

What if that's exactly how he needs you to help? a voice asked in the back of her mind.

The ledge became narrower, but just when it seemed it would peter out entirely, leaving them stranded, the Messenger stopped, pointed right—and stepped into the rock.

Kalar swore. "I told you he was a ghost!"

For a moment Amarynth thought he was right, that the Messenger had actually walked through the cliff face. But when she reached the place where he had been standing, she saw the glimmer of the trail leading into a narrow crack in the wall, barely wide enough for her to walk without turning sideways. Packed snow, frozen as hard as the rock itself, paved the passageway. She moved cautiously down it, trailing one hand against the cold stone, and suddenly saw ahead of her a new kind of light, warm and yellow: honest candlelight glowing inside the Messenger's cave.

It was not very big, not much bigger than her grandfather's Spirit Chamber. There was a pallet against the far wall, spread with grey blankets, and a rough table of black wood on which, stuck in its own wax, stood the single candle that lit the chamber. The Messenger sat in the only chair at that table, hands steepled before him, as though he had been there all night waiting for them. "So, here you are," he said as they entered. "My home, for the moment."

Amarynth tossed her pack on the hard-packed earth of the floor and sank down beside it. "Praise the One," she said.

The Messenger smiled.

Kalar stood in the doorway, hands on his hips, surveying the chamber with distaste. "Not exactly cozy."

"Kalar—" Amarynth began tiredly, but to her surprise, the Messenger laughed.

"There speaks a true Guesthost's son," he said. "Well,

lad, it's true it's not as fine as your father's establishment, but it's far better than sitting around a campfire down below fighting off Black Guards, don't you think?"

Kalar gave a noncommittal shrug, but he slipped off his own pack and set it, along with his bow and quiver, on the table. From the pack he took a lump of dry cheese and drier bread, and his water flask, which gurgled when he shook it. "I don't suppose the provisions you have are any better?"

"Alas," said the Messenger, "I lead a simple life here. At the moment my cupboard—if I had one—would be bare."

"Then you must share what we have," Kalar said firmly, and Amarynth gave him a surprised look before realizing he was making the offer out of his sense of Guesthostly duty.

"Oh, no," the Messenger said. "I have no need of food at the moment. But please, you two go ahead."

"Well enough. But the offer remains." Kalar drank from the flask and offered it to Amarynth, who accepted gratefully, suddenly aware, with some of the strain taken off her aching muscles, how thirsty she was; and then even more aware, as she handed the flask back, of hunger. She reached for her own pack and the little bit of meat and bread she still carried. Kalar took his own bread and cheese and went to the cave mouth, sitting down beside the half-melted pile of snow that had drifted through it, his drawn sword beside him.

"There's no need for that," the Messenger said

mildly. "The Black Guards and Prince Ka-Raamon will not attempt the mountain until morning."

"Humour me," Kalar said, biting into his cheese.

The Messenger chuckled, shaking his head, but his expression turned grave as he looked at Amarynth. "So," he said. "Eat, and then sleep. We have only tomorrow in which to prepare. Ka-Raamon will find this cave before nightfall; we must be ready by then."

Sleep. As he said the word, a powerful desire to do just that came over Amarynth. She had intended to question him once they reached the cave, find out who he was, and what he expected of her; how he knew what he said he knew about the prince, and everything else—but there was no denying her body's need. Covered by her cloak, she pillowed her head on the backpack and almost instantly slept.

She woke to grey light, streaming through the cave mouth over the prostrate form of Kalar, sound asleep beside his weapon. She sat up quickly, then wished she hadn't as every muscle protested the nighttime climb and the hours spent reclining on the hard floor. And then she smelled smoke, and the wonderful scent of roasting meat, and turned to see the Messenger cooking a haunch of burla over a fire whose smoke drifted up to the ceiling and vanished through a dark opening Amarynth had not noticed the night before.

She swallowed and climbed creakily to her feet, unable to stifle a groan as she did so. Kalar stirred, sat up as quickly as she had, and echoed the groan. She gave him a rueful smile, then said to the Messenger. "Good morning. Where did the meat come from?"

"The One provides," said the Messenger. "Eat well. You will need great strength today."

For what? she wanted to ask, but hunger came first, and she took the proffered meat and the fresh bread that went with it uncritically, though wondering how the Messenger had obtained either when, as he had put it, his cupboard was bare. *He must have a larder outside somewhere*, she thought, chewing and swallowing. *Anyway, there's nothing wrong with the food.*

Kalar looked at his share suspiciously when the Messenger gave it to him, but once he had tasted it, wolfed it down. When he and Amarynth had filled themselves, the Messenger, who ate nothing himself, turned grave. "Now, lad," he said to Kalar, "*now* you should keep watch. Guard the door. Anyone attacking must come at you one at a time, and there's no room to swing a sword in the passage outside. As long as you don't let them through the door, Amarynth and I will be undisturbed."

Amarynth's throat felt tight. "Undisturbed to do what?" she asked.

"To fight the Beast, of course."

Kalar looked from one to the other, then retreated to the doorway and sat down, staring out into the misty morning.

Mouth dry, Amarynth shook her head. "I can't face it again—I can't! It will swallow me—I can't stop it."

"Yes, you can," said the Messenger. "In fact, you must; you're Haven's last hope."

"*No!*" The word exploded from her. "No! I'm not a Spirit Singer—just an apprentice. I'm nothing to the Beast." She glared at the Messenger. "Fight him yourself! You're the one with all the great powers."

"Better to say I have access to great powers."

"The same thing!"

"I'm afraid not." The old man sighed. "My powers are useless against the Beast. I cannot fight him, I cannot face him."

Amarynth stared. "But—"

"I can act only in the Lower World. In the Between World, I can do nothing but cast illusions, like any other wandering spirit."

"Wandering—" Suddenly it dawned on Amarynth what the truth must be. "But—but—" She got no further.

The Messenger nodded and smiled sadly. "I see you guess my secret. I'm afraid Kalar was right: I, dear girl, am a ghost."

CHAPTER 21

Amarynth felt something pressing against her spine and realized dimly she had backed up against the cold stone of the cave wall. She was peripherally aware of Kalar rising, sword ready, unsure what was happening but ready to protect her from the Messenger, but she waved him away. *What can a blade do against a ghost?* she thought, and then felt foolish for taking the man's claim seriously, when everything she knew about spirits insisted he couldn't be telling the truth.

If it's so foolish, why are you trying to back through the wall? a cooler part of her mind interjected.

The Messenger seemed to be wondering the same thing. "Come now, Amarynth, who are you to be frightened of a ghost? You're a Spirit Singer, or at least you have the Gift. You've seen many a dead body and many a wandering spirit."

"Ghosts," said Amarynth distinctly, "have no power

in the Lower World except to frighten. And they are always tied to the remains of some slain person, someone who died unSung." She hesitated, remembering the army of spirits that had accosted them on the trail, but pressed on nonetheless. "You met us many miles from here, you climbed the mountain with us; you handle objects, put out fires, light candles—you cannot be a ghost."

The Messenger laughed. "You remember your lessons well. And everything you say is true—of most ghosts. But there are ghosts and ghosts. I am not an ordinary spirit."

"You are not a spirit at all!" Amarynth said forcefully. "I don't know what you are, except a liar."

The old man motioned to the chair she had vacated. "Won't you please sit down?" he said reasonably. "It's much harder to be fierce from a chair."

Amarynth hesitated; then, angry at her own fear, stepped forward and sat, though not comfortably.

The Messenger leaned toward her, the light of the candle twinkling in his eyes and tingeing his hair and eyebrows gold. "The ghosts you are familiar with are all but powerless, it's true, though the power to bring fear is not to be scoffed at. But that is because they are caught between two worlds—still bound to the Lower World by their decaying flesh but pulled to the Between World by their restless spirits.

"The wandering spirits of the Between World are likewise powerless in the Lower World. Having been Sung from their bodies, but failing to pass through the

Gate, they, too can only cause fear, and only in the Between World, mainly by spinning illusions. They try to lure Singers and the ones they Sing from the Path."

Amarynth stirred restlessly. "I know all this."

The Messenger raised his hand. "Please. Let me finish." He paused, then continued, "But the Between World is not really a proper place for spirits. It is a half-way-place, not a dwelling place. The poor souls trapped within it don't know what the spirit life is meant to be. That can only be found in the Upper World. And that," he spread his hands, "is where I come from."

It took a moment for his claim to register on Amarynth, then she leaped to her feet again. "Liar!" she cried. "No one has ever come back from the Upper World, except—" She stopped. "Except the Master..." She stared at the old man. There had been a drawing in her grandfather's copy of *The Master's Path*, a drawing made, during his lifetime, of the man who had been the first Spirit Singer, who had forged the first Path through the Between World, who with the help of the One had Sung all the millions of spirits that had been lost in that limbo since the creation of the world...and now she was seeing that drawing in her mind, and comparing it with the gently smiling face before her, and suddenly her knees buckled and she sat down in the chair again, hard. "Master!" she whispered.

"You look like you've seen a ghost," he said, and chuckled at his own witticism.

"You're really here," she breathed. "You've come back from the dead!"

"Not by my choice. I was sent."

"What's it like, beyond the Gate?" Amarynth asked eagerly. "Living in the presence of the One..."

The Master shook his head. "There are no words for it; it is beyond the comprehension of you who still wear flesh. You'll see for yourself someday—if you help me destroy the Beast now."

That shook her out of her reverie. "But you're the Master!" she cried. "What do you need with me?"

"I told you," he said patiently. "Master or not, I am still only a spirit, and in the Between World I am all but powerless. Worse, I would be vulnerable there; the Beast could take me as he has taken so many others, and I would swell him to the point where he might be too strong to ever be destroyed." He rubbed one hand slowly over the table's smooth surface. "But he would still be hungry, as he is now. Already he is stirring up war in Haven, faction against faction. If he is not stopped, the whole land will run red with blood...again."

"Again?" Amarynth stared at him. "This has happened before?"

The Master's hand stopped moving; clenched into a fist for a moment, then relaxed. He drew it back under the table. "Your ancestors came to Haven fleeing war," he said. "War caused by the Beast. But he was overeager in those days; he exerted his power into the Lower World before he was nearly as strong as he is now. The greatest

Spirit Singers fled their land, and from their boats they joined together and went into the Between World and broke him, freeing all the captive souls from which he drew his energy, diminishing him and driving him away, until he was little more than a memory. But in his final rage his servants killed every living person left in the Old Land, and then themselves."

"No wonder there are no records," Amarynth whispered, then gave the Master a sharp look. "So how did the Beast come back?"

"Ar-Naathon." The Master shook his head. "He found an ancient scroll overlooked during the First Landers' attempt to wipe out all memory of the Beast. And Ar-Naathon has the Singer's Gift more strongly than anyone who has ever lived—myself included. He searched the Between World, calling for the Beast. Eventually, it came. It linked with him—became, in a sense, the spirit filling his body. And the rest—the rest you have already heard."

Amarynth sat silent. Before her sat the First Singer, the Master, the one the common people thought of in the same breath as the One, and even Singers sometimes came close to venerating, though they knew he had been a man like any other. Yet he was telling her that Ar-Naathon was more powerful than even he had been—and that she was the one who must stand in his way. It was ludicrous. "Then what can we do?" she finally burst out. "If Ar-Naathon is stronger than even you, he'll crush me and suck me dry. Nothing can stop him!"

"You're wrong," said the Master intensely. "True, Ar-Naathon is strong, and he also has the power of the Beast to draw on. But I am no longer as I was. Although I do not have the power I once had—"

"Then we're helpless!"

"Peace!" For the first time there was a trace of anger in the Master's voice, and it seemed to shake the room. When he spoke again it was with sternness approaching majesty. "I am not flesh, and the Gift is for those who breathe. But I am filled with the power of the Upper World, with as much of the Light of the One as my poor spirit can bear. All I need is a way to channel that power into the Between World. I need someone who can enter the Between World and act effectively there. I need you!"

Amarynth swallowed. "I don't think I can do it. The Beast..." Her voice trailed off.

The Master's tone softened. "You can. I read that in you, Amarynth. You do what you must. You always have."

It seemed to Amarynth the room had filled with a deep chill, the breath of the spirit world, but though she trembled, she said, "All right."

The Master nodded gravely. "It is well," he said. "Your part will simply be to—" Suddenly he stiffened. "Black Guards!"

Kalar leaped to his feet. "Where?"

"On the cliff trail. *No*, young fool!" Too late; Kalar was gone.

Amarynth stood to go after him, but the Master

stopped her with a look. "They have come sooner than I thought. It is time."

Amarynth turned back to him. "What do I do?" she whispered.

"Sit." She did, and he moved the candle closer to her, pushing aside Kalar's bow.

"He should have taken that with him," she said, but the Master hushed her.

"Enter the Between World," he told her. "I will be holding your hands. I do not think you'll have to search for the Beast; he is hovering over us. As, I might add, is Ar-Naathon."

"This far from Havenheart?"

"I told you; he uses his son. Ar-Naathon's body lies next to death in his many-windowed tower; almost all of his spirit is in Ka-Raamon, who climbs the trail toward us. Ar-Naathon and the Beast both know that this is Haven's last hope to withstand them, child."

"And a poor one," Amarynth muttered.

"Untrue," the Master said sharply. "I will fill you with the might of the One Himself, once you enter the Between World. You will find yourself on a Path, a Path which I forged here before the Beast was as strong as he now is. The Beast will block that Path. You must tread it nonetheless, using the power I provide to bore through the Beast's darkness. If you can pass him, you will destroy him, for beyond lies the Gate, and if that opens at his back, the souls he has devoured will be torn away from him and he will shrink into nothingness once more."

"But I'm just an apprentice! I've never been to the Gate. I can't open it!"

"My child, if you reach the Gate filled with the power of the One, do you really think it will fail to open?"

There was a thunder of falling rock outside, and Amarynth half-turned; but the Master reached out and seized her hands. Ghost or not, his fingers were warm on her skin. "Young Kalar is still safe," he reassured her. "He only watches, learning, as does the prince, that I am not totally defenceless. I have an army, which I believe you met."

"The ghostly horde!" Amarynth stared at him. "I wondered how they could exist here so far from where their bodies must lie. But they have no power..."

"Even less than usual, against the soulless Black Guards," the Master agreed. "The Black Guards feel no fear. But they are easily misled. Even now, they follow phantoms to destruction. With luck, not one will reach the cave."

"Ramon—" In her mind's eye Amarynth saw that proud blonde head bloodied and lifeless, and despite what the Master had told her about the prince, she mourned him.

"Ka-Raamon will not be caught so easily," the Master said gravely. "Not instilled with the combined might of his father and the Beast. Should he reach the cave before we are done—then we must trust to Kalar's sword to keep him at bay long enough for our task to be completed. But I tell you now, Amarynth—whatever happens, you must not leave the Between World once we begin. And you must not break contact with me. I must touch you to transfer my power. Release my hands or flee the Beast once you have begun the attack, and Haven is lost."

Amarynth swallowed but nodded. "I understand."

"Good." He gave her a small smile. "Then let us begin."

Amarynth focused on the candle flame, breathing deeply, trying to ignore the rapid pounding of her pulse.

The cavern walls faded around her.

CHAPTER 22

Amarynth stood where she had thought she would never stand again, on the grey plain of the Between World, a Path soaring above her. The mountains were invisible here, though the walls and contents of the cave itself had shadowy substance.

Timara was instantly with her, crying piteously, and Amarynth gathered the tiny spirit close and comforted her. But beside her, where she should have seen the form and spirit of the Master, there was nothing.

Yet she could feel him, feel power coursing into her, power such as she had never imagined. With ease she shifted perspective so that she stood on the Path; and then she saw the Beast.

It had grown immeasurably since the last time she faced it, in the Temple of the One. It not only stretched across the Path, swallowing it, it extended above and below and to either side so far she could not see its limits.

Black as midnight though it was, it seemed to pulse with waves of even deeper darkness, as though a giant heart somewhere deep within beat waves of power through it. Timara's spirit shrank almost to invisibility, and the spark of her own spirit flickered. For a moment the walls of the cave solidified around her as terror drove her back into her body. But then the Master's power swelled within her, strengthening her soul, setting it ablaze with light such as she had never imagined.

She readied herself to move forward...but before she could take her first step, the Beast roared and descended upon her like an avalanche of night.

She screamed soundlessly as foulness enveloped her. Even the light of the Path vanished, and her spirit, blazing so brightly a moment before, shrank to the merest pinprick of light, like a tiny star, sheltering Timara invisibly inside.

But that spark did not go out, nor was it swallowed by the vast sea of fury and hatred surrounding her, emotions she sensed so strongly they seemed her own—and, ironically, helped give her the strength to fight back.

She reached for power, reached for everything the Master could give her, and poured it into the flickering flame of her soul, strengthening it, building it, making it swell from a tiny star to a burning planet to a glowing moon, driving away the darkness until once more she blazed like the sun itself.

Slowly her illusory Between World body surrounded that spirit, transparent as glass, then filled, bit by bit, as though with fog, and finally took on solidity. Around her the cave's outline came clear, though blackness still raged outside it, and at her feet a faint glimmering appeared, a glimmering that soaked up the light of her power and, strengthening, began slowly to extend outward.

The Path, she thought; and took her first step upon it.

Impotent rage swirled through the Beast's dark substance. Bolts of blue fire lanced at her but shattered against the Master's light. Monsters from her worst nightmares leaped and gibbered in the periphery of her vision but faded into nothingness when she looked straight at them, for no illusion could withstand the clear light the Master poured into her from the Upper World.

She took another step, and another. Each felt like walking in wet snow that clung to and weighted her feet, but with each step the snow became less deep. The Beast howled. She felt the first twinge of its fear, and her spirit blazed even brighter.

The sketchy substance of the cave dwindled behind her. The Path stretched back to it straight and unsullied by the Beast's darkness, and ahead she thought she saw a thinning of the midnight gloom. *Yes*, she heard, the faintest hint of a whisper from the Master. *Keep pushing. You're almost through. You've almost won...*

But then she felt a surge of savage glee within the Beast, and some distant impulse from her body made her look back.

Tiny and far away she saw the cavern, like a child's

toy. Just inside the door stood the shadowy shape of Kalar, sword drawn, facing—

Facing Prince Ka-Raamon, whose shadow-form was filled, not with a spirit light, but with the blackness of the Beast. Even as Amarynth watched, their swords clashed, and Kalar's flew from his grasp. The boy fell backward, and Ka-Raamon stepped forward, blade raised.

Amarynth stopped on the Path. *Kalar!* she screamed silently.

You mustn't stop! the Master whispered. *You must move forward. Only a little farther. If you stop you'll lose ground. You'll never be able to break through!*

But Amarynth hardly heard him. She was remembering all the times Kalar had saved her—on the Crag, from the Wanderers, on Icethorn itself—and suddenly the Beast seemed unimportant. Kalar's life was all that mattered.

Amarynth, no! the Master cried, but it was too late.

Like a bolt of lightning, Amarynth, still power-filled, rushed back down the path and into her body, hearing the laughter of the Beast fading behind her, and the despairing, repeated cry of the Master, *No!*

Her eyes flicked open. She lunged forward and seized Kalar's bow from the table, nocking an arrow as she spun around. The fading power of the Master, who fell back from her limp and white, eyes closed, gave her a burst of unnatural speed. In an instant she faced the prince, standing with raised sword over Kalar, who stared up at him with wide eyes in a pale face.

"Put the sword down," Amarynth commanded, bow drawn, arrow aimed at the prince's heart.

The blonde head came up in surprise, and then Ka-Raamon's mouth twisted in a sardonic grin that tugged at her heart with memories of their journey together. "How nice of you to come back, Amarynth," he said. "I missed you. Why did you run out on me yesterday?"

"You betrayed us," she said. "You went to get the Black Guards."

"Black Guards?" The prince raised an eyebrow. "I don't see any Black Guards. I came back from my walk and you were gone."

"Your Black Guards fell to their deaths," Kalar spat out. "Don't listen to him, Amarynth."

The prince ignored him. "If there were Black Guards around, then I can understand why you fled the fire," he said, "but I assure you I had nothing to do with them. The first I knew of your distrust was when Kalar attacked me on the ledge. I was lucky he didn't send me over."

"I said, put the sword down," Amarynth repeated. A tiny shiver ran through the arm holding the bow drawn.

"You put down the bow, I'll put down the sword," said the prince reasonably. "Come now, Amarynth, you're not my enemy. You've been listening to Kalar's lies —and I don't know what tales that old man back there has been filling your head with, but if they make you aim a shaft at me..." He smiled. "I've never been anything but your friend, Amarynth. And I hoped to be more, remember?"

Amarynth breath came in ragged gasps. "I have seen you, Ka-Raamon. I've seen you from the Between World. I've seen the blackness filling you. You're not even the prince. You're his father. Ar-Naathon and the Beast fill that body, not Ramon."

The prince's smile slipped a little. "The old man *has* been lying to you. No one can fill another's body with his spirit. Put the bow down, we can talk..."

"No!"

Ka-Raamon held out his hand and took a step toward her. "Come on, Amarynth. Think. Even if this impossible thing were true, and my father's spirit were here, you wouldn't be killing him. You'd be killing me. *Me*, Amarynth. Ramon. Your friend. Remember that glorious flowered field we crossed hand in hand? Remember how you laughed at my story of the time the bee swarm got into the temple?" He took another step. "That's who you'd be killing. Not my father." Another step. "Give me the bow, Amarynth."

He was within three steps of her now. *I can't kill him,* she thought despairingly. *I can't. He's just a boy. He was my friend. He said he loved me. I almost loved him...*

Another two steps and she would lose the opportunity. She started to relax the tension on the string.

Kalar lunged for his sword.

With inhuman speed Ka-Raamon rounded on him, blade lashing out, scoring Kalar's arm. The younger boy gasped and scrambled away, white-faced, clutching the wound, blood welling over his fingers, and the prince stepped after him, grinning savagely. He lifted his sword to split Kalar's skull—

—and Amarynth's arrow buried itself in his back with such force the point burst through his chest in a spray of scarlet.

The prince gave a choking, gasping cry. His sword dropped from his hand. He fell to his knees, hands scrabbling uselessly at the arrowhead, then collapsed on his side, coughing blood.

Amarynth flung the bow away in horror and knelt beside him. "Ramon, I'm sorry!" she cried.

Something changed in his face. It had been shrewd, hard; suddenly it was the face of a boy again, and Amarynth knew that Ar-Naathon's spirit was no longer in control—that the one dying before her was only her friend, Ramon.

Her friend, whom she had just killed.

"I—I'm sorry," he said weakly. Bloodstained fingers seized her hand. "I never wanted...to hurt...but my father..."

"I understand," she whispered.

Ramon grimaced in pain, then choked out, "You still have a chance. My father—I am holding him here. Inside me. He is trying to return to his own body. If you go into the Between World, keep him there until I...until I am dead...I don't think he will be able to return."

"You mean he'll die, too?"

"Yes...but more, I—" He coughed, and fresh blood spattered the earthen floor. "No time," he gasped. "Go, go now—"

There was no time for candle flame or meditation. Amarynth closed her eyes and flung herself into the Between World by brute force.

At once, she saw the prince had spoken truth. He lay before her in the Between World as he had in the Lower World, his spirit tugging to be free of his dying body, but bound there yet…

And also bound, by a visible cord of blackness, was the spirit of Ar-Naathon.

Amarynth knew it was he, though he had no body. In her Singer's vision, he was a seething dark star, as black with the power of the Beast as her own soul had been white with the power of the Master.

She wished she had some of that power now, but it was gone, lost when she turned back to save Kalar. *And kill Ramon*, she thought, but suppressed it brutally. She had no time now for guilt or remorse; that would come later.

With the Master's power she was sure she could have held Ar-Naathon easily, for he was far from his body and weakened by distance and shock. Yet without the Master filling her, he was still far more powerful than she.

There was only one way she knew of to bind him to her long enough—only one way she knew of to bind *any* spirit in the Between World.

She began to Sing.

Her own spirit strengthened as she did so, and gradually the lines of power reached out, enfolding the black star that was Ar-Naathon, and the flicker that was the prince, and the spark that was Timara, who had returned to her once more. As she continued to Sing, and the power continued to build, she realized that she had already gone beyond her own capabilities—that the Master was with her again, not as strong as before, but still helping her, linked to her as the others were, through her Song.

And then, Ka-Raamon died.

Amarynth felt a powerful tug as Ar-Naathon made a last, frantic attempt to flee back to his own body, so powerful she knew she would have broken without the Master's help. But her bonds held, and she felt Ar-Naathon's faint connection with his own body part and wither, lost forever, and knew that back in his many-windowed tower, high above Havenheart, he, too, lay dead.

Thunder above her, the thunder of a thousand storms. She looked up into the blackness of the Beast— and saw it coming apart.

Lightning blazed from end to end of the Beast's darkness, like huge rents appearing in funeral velvet, and then the whole black sky crazed like shattering glass, and there was another roar—a vast, exultant shout of freedom.

Quickly, whispered the Master. *Onto the Path!*

Amarynth stepped onto that glimmering roadway, now stretching straight as an arrow into infinity, and with speed born of the Master's power, flashed along it, still Singing.

She became aware first of a familiar, shy presence —*Davin*, she realized. He attached himself to the streaming comet of light she had become. But he was only the first.

From all over the Between World they flowed to her, all the spirits that had been lost in the Darkness of the Beast—simple men and women of the villages, soldiers of the city, other Spirit Singers who had not become Wanderers. She felt a warm presence on the edge of the vast throng and realized it was her grandfather, radiating pride and love like a beacon, and indescribable joy filled her heart.

The spirits of those who had become Black Guards joined to her, and the spirits who had made up the Master's ghostly army, accompanying the prince beyond his journey's end, even as they had promised. The spirits of those who had died defending the warren in Haven-heart were there, including that of Mythos, the Singer who had sent her out—all those whom the Beast had taken.

And finally, ahead of her, she saw light—golden, like the sun but more glorious, like the moon but more beautiful, like starlight but more pure. It hung like a veil across the Path, and she knew it at once for the Gate.

The vast throng slowed, just a moment; and then suddenly their bonds to her dissolved and they rushed headlong into the Light, while she slowed and finally stopped, watching them stream away from her, a strange, bittersweet grief mingling with her joy.

Timara was one of the last to go, her lonesome crying stilled at last, her clear child-laugh ringing out and warming Amarynth's heart as she raced into the Upper World. After that, only she and the spirit of Ka-Raamon remained, and the black horror of Ar-Naathon, now shrunk to a pinprick of darkness.

The prince's spirit hesitated an instant longer, and Amarynth felt flowing from it regret and—her spirit brightened—love. But then the pull of the Light grew too strong and he, too, was gone.

Thus, finally, there was only Ar-Naathon. For a long moment he hung there, a tiny, writhing point of evil; and then suddenly he fled the Path, streaking away into the infinite void of the Between World, tormented by the Light he could never join.

The Gate diminished, shrinking in upon itself until it had the appearance of a door through which streamed the light of warm hearths and glowing lamps, promising comfort and safety, as though she had just come home to a cozy cottage through the cold and dark of a winter storm.

Someone stood in that light, and Amarynth, moving a little closer, saw it was the Master, as solid and real-seeming as he had been in the Lower World. "Not what I expected," he said wryly. "But effective."

"I had to save Kalar," Amarynth said. "I couldn't let him die. But I killed Ramon..."

"You did what you had to." The Master smiled. "Like always."

"What will happen in the Lower World now?"

"There will be a bit of chaos for a while, especially in the city," he said. "New City Elders will have to be found, and there is going to be a shortage of Singers for a while, although some of the Wanderers will now return to the true path. Others, alas, have lost their Gift entirely. A few may even choose to die and join Ar-Naathon—out there." He glanced into the darkness beyond the Path.

"I still don't understand what happened. Why did the Beast dissolve?"

"The Beast can only take shape when it has an outlet into the Lower World," said the Master. "Like everything else, it is powerless in the Between World without a body —or bodies—to draw power from. It was bound to many bodies in the Lower World, but Ar-Naathon was the one who had summoned it. He was like the keystone of an arch. When he died, with no one to take his place, the Beast could no longer hold on to all the spirits it had absorbed. It fell apart."

"Then we're rid of it forever?"

The Master smiled sadly. "Only for the time being. It's always out there, waiting, looking for an opening into the Lower World. But, with the One's help, it will wait another five hundred years—or longer." His smile brightened again. "And you? Where will *you* go now?"

"Home," Amarynth replied simply. "Covedrift. The elders are waiting."

"Then let that be my parting gift to you," said the Master. "Farewell, Amarynth Spirit Singer!"

And suddenly the Gate was rushing away from her, dwindling to a golden spark and then to nothing, while beneath her the grey plain of the border of the Lower World swelled—and finally, her body welcomed her back.

Amarynth opened her eyes—then closed them, opened them again, and finally rubbed them, hard.

The cavern had vanished.

Instead, she lay on soft grass beneath a lonely, wind-warped tree. Overhead, the sky was blue and dotted with slowly drifting, fluffy white clouds; a single bird rode the breeze and made a sound like a crying child.

That's a sea-karil! She sat up sharply.

She lay at the base of a hill dotted with a few trees and many rocks. Behind her rose a distant blue range of mountains; in front of her rose—she blinked, but the image wouldn't go away.

In front of her rose her grandfather's tower.

In front of her also rose Kalar, who stood up from the boulder on which he had been seated and looked down at her with a bemused expression. Dried blood still covered his sleeve and tunic, but the flesh of his arm, visible beneath the torn cloth, seemed undamaged except for a faint scar. He held out his hand to help her to her feet, and as she stood she asked, "What happened?"

"I was hoping you could tell me," he said. "I saw you kill the prince, but after that I passed out. From the wound in my arm." He glanced down and touched the scar. "When I woke up a moment ago, the wound was gone, and we were here." He looked up again, and then around. "Wherever 'here' is."

"This is my home," Amarynth said, still only half-believing it herself. "That's my grandfather's tower; Covedrift is just the other side of the hill. But how did we —" Suddenly she remembered the Master's last mysterious mention of a gift, and his question, *Where will you go now?*

She looked at Kalar's arm. It appeared the Master had had a gift for each of them.

"Then those aren't the Haunted Mountains," Kalar said wonderingly. "They're the Northern Range. *My* mountains."

Amarynth nodded.

Kalar's face hardened. "And still filled with Wanderers and Black Guards and—"

"No." Amarynth shook her head. "That's all done, Kalar. Ar-Naathon is dead. So are the Black Guards. And the Wanderers have lost their power." She smiled a little timorously. "We did it."

Kalar snorted. "*You* did it. I just came along to protect

you." But then his expression softened. "Although, there at the end—"

Amarynth reached out and touched the scar on his arm. "Thank you."

Kalar put his hand over hers for a moment, looking into her eyes, then suddenly turned away and picked up his pack from the ground behind him. "Well, I suppose I had better be going," he said gruffly. "It's a long walk to Snowdeep."

Amarynth turned and looked at those distant mountains, then back at Kalar. "Why don't you stay here?" she said impulsively. "For a while, at least."

He turned to her slowly. "Here?"

"Your family is dead. There's nothing for you in your old village."

"There's the Guesthouse." But Kalar looked thoughtful. "Although I don't much care to associate with the cowards who let my father be slain in the street."

"So don't go back," Amarynth urged. "Stay here. It's a good village."

"But it doesn't have a Spirit Singer."

She smiled at him.

"Does it?" he said.

For answer, Amarynth pulled her Emblem from beneath her clothes. Even in the bright sunshine it blazed with purple light. "Yes," she said. "It does."

Kalar blinked at it, then at her. "Well, then," he said. "I guess it has everything."

Amarynth held out her hand to him. "Changed your mind about 'Death Squawkers'?"

Kalar took her hand, his fingers warm and strong around hers. "Some of them," he said, "have their good points."

THE END

Edward Willett is the author of more than sixty books of science fiction, fantasy, and non-fiction for readers of all ages. *Marseguro* (DAW Books) won the Aurora Award (honouring the best in Canadian science fiction and fantasy) for Best Long-Form Work in English in 2009. His young adult fantasy *Spirit Singer* (this book!) won the Regina Book Award for best book by a Regina author at the 2002 Saskatchewan Book Awards. Several other of his books have been shortlisted for those and other awards.

Ed's tenth novel for DAW, *Worldshaper* (September 2018), launched a new fantasy/science fiction series, *Worldshapers*. Book 2, *Master of the World*, comes out in September 2019. Other recent titles include *The Cityborn* and the *Masks of Aygrima* trilogy (written as E.C. Blake) for DAW, the *Peregrine Rising* duology for Bundoran Press, and the five-book *Shards of Excalibur* young-adult fantasy series for Coteau Books. His non-fiction runs the gamut from science books to biographies to history.

Born in Silver City, New Mexico, Ed moved to

Saskatchewan from Texas at the age of eight, and grew up in Weyburn, where his father taught at Western Christian College. He earned a B.A. in journalism from Harding University in Searcy, Arkansas, and returned to Weyburn to begin his career at the weekly *Weyburn Review*, first as a reporter/photographer/columnist/cartoonist, and eventually as news editor. He moved to Regina in 1988 as communications officer for the then-fledgling Saskatchewan Science Centre. He began writing full-time in 1993.

For two decades Ed wrote a weekly science column that appeared in the *Regina Leader Post* and other newspapers; an audio version ran weekly on CBC Saskatchewan's *Afternoon Edition* for most of that time. He has also appeared on CBC TV nationally to talk about science topics.

In addition to being a writer, Ed is a professional actor and singer who has performed in numerous plays, musicals, and operas, and sung in several auditioned choirs. He lives in Regina, Saskatchewan, with his wife, Margaret Anne Hodges, P. Eng., a past president of the Association of Professional Engineers and Geoscientists of Saskatchewan, and their teenaged daughter, Alice.

You can find Ed online at www.edwardwillett.com.

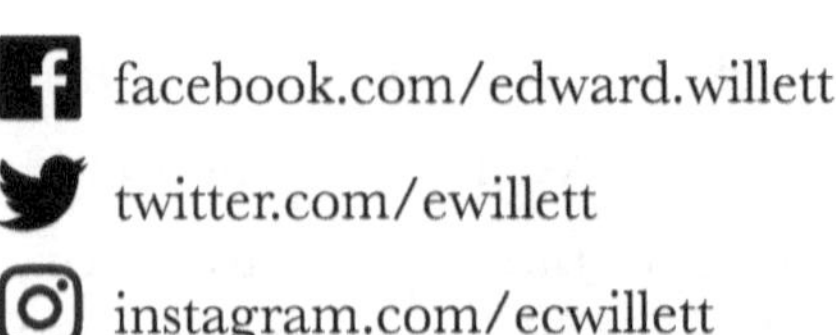

From Bundoran Press

PEREGRINE RISING

Right to Know

Falcon's Egg

From Coteau Books

THE SHARDS OF EXCALIBUR

Song of the Sword

Twist of the Blade

Lake in the Clouds

Cave Beneath the Sea

Door into Faerie

From Shadowpaw Press

Paths to the Stars: Twenty-two Fantastical Tales of Imagination

From Your Nickel's Worth Publishing

I Tumble through the Diamond Dust: A Collection of Fantastical Poems